Vanity Unfair

THE SLOVAK LIST

Vanity Unfair

ZUZANA CIGÁNOVÁ

TRANSLATED BY
MAGDALENA MULLEK

LONDON NEW YORK CALCUTTA

The Slovak List
SERIES EDITOR: Julia Sherwood

This book was published with financial support from SLOLIA,
Centre for Information on Literature, Bratislava.

The translator thanks

u. fond
na podporu
umenia

Supported using public funding by the Slovak Arts Council.

Seagull Books, 2022

Originally published in Slovak as *Špaky v tŕní*

Original text © Zuzana Cigánová, 2012

English translation © Magdalena Mullek, 2022

First published in English translation by Seagull Books, 2022

ISBN   978 1 80309 082 5

British Library Cataloguing-in-Publication Data

A catalogue record for this book is available from the British Library

Typeset by Seagull Books, Calcutta, India

Printed and bound in the USA by Integrated Books International

In the lives of the good, bad people are the deciding factor. That's just how it goes. In the lives of the bad, the good ones disappear. They don't even notice them.

She knew there was trouble. So she kept oh-so-quiet . . . She was like a little shadow. A little light breeze that goes around doing what needs to be done. With a tiny smile. As quiet as a mouse. She barely breathed . . . She didn't get in the way, didn't ask questions, didn't marvel at anything, she didn't even look at him that much. And she certainly didn't want anything . . . She just wanted . . . to hold onto every minute, every fraction of a moment, every split second. Because it was already trembling. It was already melting, it was weeping like rain. It only held together on the honour system. Except that he . . . He wasn't enjoying it there any more. There didn't interest him any more. There bothered him. Even at midnight, in the middle of the night . . . He didn't even look at her face when they bumped into one another. He just tapped her on the shoulder, move, and went by . . . One time they got tangled up, both right, both left, and then he squeezed by her the way one does by a dirty car—stomach sucked in, arms up. At that, a tear welled up in her eye . . .

He kept reading the paper, turning the TV on, turning the TV off. One time he started to whistle, but the moment she looked like she was enjoying it, he stopped. It was terribly loud for that stiff apartment . . . All day Saturday he only said—no, thank you (to more potatoes), no, I wouldn't (like some coffee), and 'night

3

(to good night) . . . Truth be told, she preferred to be elsewhere, and she always had something to do. So that he wouldn't have to do anything he didn't want to. Since he didn't even want to anything . . . It never crossed her mind that he could be bored. In that zealous zeal of hers, in that crazed craze of hers, in that insufferable suffering of hers . . . In the morning he said he had work to do, but with a smile, and she was happy, even though it was Sunday. He had a very nice smile. A vulnerable smile. She kept looking at his mouth . . . And she said, I know, I know, of course, no problem—she just wanted to keep the peace . . . Just to belong somewhere a little while longer. For a few more days, in case someone came over. Before it was completely clear that no one would be coming. Already. To everyone . . . Just as a vacation. Just to have the experience. Just to make summer last a little longer. Just to see the sea one more time . . . And then she could go back home. To loneliness. She didn't have more in her anyway. Nor the money . . .

She just wanted to remember it. That good mood in the morning, that pleasure of stretching, yawning. That unexpected grab by the back—enough lazing around! It always startled her a little, it always made her a little sad . . . But pulling off those pajamas with one hand, in one fell swoop, that handsome peek, that boyish shock of hair ready for wind or rain, made up for it in spades . . . The two moans of the jeans, each trouser leg creaking hard, that caress in the middle, still there . . . all those curved shadows, golden light on the chest, the arms, the thighs, that warmth, that body she wished not to forget . . . Because her husband was a gorgeous man!

And all those tastes and smells and breaths and sighs when they made love. She wished to inscribe them . . . Into everything she had. Into the palms of her hands, into her. Into the throat she barely had, those few dizzying kisses. Because she knew she'd only be looking from now on—window shopping—and imagining . . . When a man helps a woman with her coat. When he fixes a strand of her hair, when he holds the door for her, for real, so that it doesn't hit her, with his hand on her back the whole time, so gently that she doesn't even know it's there. He must feel her, he must have her, he always wants . . . And he can't help turning around to see if everyone knows, that she's only his, that he's the only one . . . But she didn't complain, she was glad that she got to experience it, she too got to belong somewhere. She got to be where dinner is made, as usual, the same thing as always. Where you have Christmas jitters, like every year, wondering how Aunt Nada's chocolate balls would turn out. And she got to have someone on the other side of the door while she was bathing . . . God knows why, she didn't want to be home alone while bathing. All she really wanted was to be home. Behind a door, locked for the night. Where you take off your bra, rip it out of all the sweaty creases . . .

Except that now she even slept in it, and Christmas was hopelessly far away. She wasn't stupid, just ugly. Damn the whole thing. So plainly, that it wasn't worth talking about. So indefinitely, that nothing could be done about it. Except turn out the lights . . . What can you do with short arms, short legs, a broad torso, a nonexistent butt, and even smaller, greasy hillocks of breasts . . . Small breasts, but big paws. Everything's connected! Wretched teeth and ditto hair. When they were little, her brother used to say that her hair was pf! Super light, super fine. And that was how it stayed. Pf, contempt worthy. Constantly matted, so-called perma-oily . . . Her childhood immunity, on the other hand, didn't stay. People had stopped saying long ago, she'll grow out of it, she'll pull through, you know how ugly Marilyn Monroe was . . . But unlike M. M., she just got fat. Cellulite covered her like bark, which didn't allow the bones to grow. She was wide and short. Like a trashcan. Like a waste basket, neither tits nor ass . . . Every now and then she probably said to herself, no one likes me, and she downed a box of bonbons. She tossed a bon bomb into that garbage bin. And sometimes she threw it up, and sometimes she didn't. Depending on whether she was just desperate or she didn't care any more . . . But that only happened rarely nowadays. Not that she wasn't desperate, but she cared. She didn't have time, she had a child . . .

And she had a husband she didn't have. So it only happened at night. When the baby was asleep, and he didn't come home. He simply didn't come home, she'd say out loud, wipe her eyes, and have some. No one likes me anyway. Was the name of that box of bonbons. But she did, so she went to throw up. Paralympians have it worse—she'd tell herself over the toilet—at least I have him. Stupid heart. Naive to the point of moronism. It didn't get lopped off, it's just broken . . . She would have never believed it could happen in such an ordinary way, such an everyday way, such a kitchen way, that thing which is in books and the movies. And out of her broken heart poured love for both of them. And enough for all three, because the baby was still little and didn't know any better . . . She drank up the occasion, all the way, bottoms up. She was enjoying it and that was that. Every infinitesimal instant. Every bittersweet second . . .

He knew how to live too. He was an athlete, body and soul. Tennis, skiing. Presently he was switching to snowboarding. Golf was something he only watched on TV for now. Individual sports, that was his thing. Including . . . And he must have been good. They wanted seconds. All of them. He didn't. Another day, another play. Plenty of pussy to choose from . . . Soccer he only played occasionally, just for fun, so as not to break up the group. It was what he kept going back to, where he had friends, where he had always belonged. He was at his best in the locker room. The locker room was his turf! It didn't matter who won. Elegantly hot, sexily exhausted, he even did some breathing exercises. Showered to perfection, ready to go, he tossed his fabulous gear into his fabulous bag with one hand tied behind his back. He enjoyed that, that was his thing. The right stuff in the right place. Nike gear on a Nike body! He had the biggest one. Definitely. No contest. He didn't even bother checking any more. He liked it when there was a mirror in the locker room. He had excellent peripheral vision. He often said so. He often said, us guys, and, a real man wouldn't even break a sweat, and, a man needs it. What he couldn't have, he didn't need. What he didn't know, didn't exist. Or it was useless. Who gives a shit. Like when Cyril and Methodius came! You're so funny, Paťo . . . Whenever he made a mistake, he didn't correct himself. He smiled until it blew over and then he went back to talking. As infallibly as before. The right perspective, in sports and in life . . . A not-too-demanding job. They're all idiots there. And how does a man know that he has made the right decision? The only right decision is one you can take back. He earned money for the things he needed. With one hand tied behind his back. And for tips. He didn't drink much, couldn't afford it. Nor could his digestion. He wasn't stupid, just good looking . . .

She was never into putting on makeup, dressing up, showing off. For obvious reasons. It didn't improve matters. Things didn't get better, they just got colourful. Besides, no one cared. Maybe at first glance, but she had no desire to be the entertainment. And she would have had to look in the mirror. All in all, she preferred to stay home. Ever since she could remember . . . Take care of the basics, and go home. Skippety skip, dickety dick. She had no idea where she had picked up that ditty. Somewhere early on, before she knew what it was. And for a long time after that, how it was. Because she and her mother didn't have one at home. She and her awful mother didn't have one at home. And now she had one. At home. A little like exotic fruit.

And she had a dream. She dreamed that it was winter. Fragile trees were vanishing in the steel air. In rows, side by side, one after another, in every direction they were disappearing in the fog. A little bigger than shrubs, not much bigger than her. She too was chilled to the bone, and she didn't know why she was there. She rubbed her eyes . . . something was hanging on the trees. Cheerfully bright, up close as well as from the fog. But it's wintertime . . . She reached, the fruit was warm, moist, defenceless. Hard and soft. It smelled like horse chestnut flowers and tasted like seawater.

As usual, first he was surprised by how ugly she was. She was surprisingly ugly, he wasn't used to seeing women like that. His sensors were just not attuned to it. For many years he and his buddies had been tuning them at a minimum for Cs, pussy nice and high off the ground . . . And then he didn't understand. For a long time. At all. First, that there was a baby, and then, that she wanted to keep it. And their knees gave way, and they sat down on a short wall . . . This wasn't his area of expertise. In his area of expertise things were counted in games and goals, and the women were supposed to take care of their things. That was what he had been taught. He enjoyed himself when they had choices and he got to pick. And he liked it when they put it on. He was proud. They hadn't counted on it, being quite so big. A great problem to have. Quite a regular one. He had jokes ready for it. Always the same ones. The pussies were different. And they laughed like they were being paid for it. A first-rate mood before first-rate screwing . . . And when there was no mention of it, it was clear that she had it taken care of in some other way—the pussy . . . And his job was to be funny again in order to step over, to skip over those minutes when it crosses everyone's mind that it's not proper until after the wedding. He had a bit of a Christian upbringing. Or at least after I love you, that was in the movies. He had jokes for that too. Always the same ones. But most of all, he was always good looking . . . Even now. While he's making excuses, Pipina thought. She kept looking at his mouth . . . And she realized that it was true, that he wasn't ready. That he didn't have it in him. That it was a goof. A goofie, she corrected him. Let's call him Goofie, OK? He simply didn't know what to do, so he simply left. He was simply gone, that was how simple it was . . . Actually, he forgot about it. Athletes practice that. As part of their training. It's all in the head. Dismiss stupid goofs, unnecessary off-pissings, near-miss spears. They don't get worked up so they can get a good night's sleep. Good rest is key. It's paramount. So that tomorrow they can perform again.

And she felt faint. She got terribly scared. Paralyzed. She only wished for one thing, to be little. So as not to have to make any decisions. Only to eat, poop, cry . . . It was actually no one's fault. They were just in the wrong place at the wrong time. And like a big wave, it had done with them as it pleased. A wave rolled in, and she fainted for a moment. The wave receded, and they were stunned, reverent, exhausted. The way one feels when nature has demonstrated who's boss. They straightened out their arms and legs and opened their eyes. She put on a T-shirt, in a flash . . . and he left. He had mentioned that he was in a hurry. That he should have already been there . . . And she hugged herself and was proud. She was beside herself because she now knew what all the fuss was about. What the fuss is always about . . .

And she had an unforgettable dream too. In a warm, velvety twilight, a few dark, friendly trees surrounded her. Like family . . . Slowly, their huge white flowers were falling off, dripping down under their own weight. Large lilies. They were mature. They were falling through the dense air and bumping into branches, into hard leaves, until at last they landed on the ground. They bounced once or twice, in slow motion, in silence, until they settled down. Big and beautiful like those up top. And they looked and smelled even better than the ones above, because they were dying . . . More and more of them kept falling through the nearly solid air, and they got caught on a spider web. A flowery curtain gleamed in the velvety darkness up to the heels of the tree. White chalices strewn every which way faintly reflected the moonlight. And their scent was strong enough to make you faint. A beautiful death.

He didn't understand it. Once he remembered. It's all in the head. And he marvelled. He was always marvelling when he was around her, though he wasn't having a good time. He remembered how he had briefly felt tender. Stunned. Hard. Pato, you're a rock . . . He remembered the wave. The kind that comes once every twenty? forty? eighty? of the regular, small ones. And for a second he was reverent again . . . Ocean waves have an inexplicable rhythm too. Maybe a lunar one, probably following the moon, he looked up . . . And everyone else looked up. He was never alone. What for.

She didn't understand it. She wasn't embarrassed at all. And she didn't care that she was ugly. For the first time since the end of her childhood, she wasn't thinking about how ugly she was. She just listened whether she was baking. Whether she was baking nicely. In an inexplicable rhythm. Maybe a lunar one, probably following the moon, she looked up. She was like an oven, but not stupid, excited. She told him so. Even the part about the oven . . . She found him again. Because she didn't care that she was ugly. Because she had enough strength for two. And he hesitated. He just hesitated, and it didn't quite register for him. Something like that can't really register. I'll watch Wimbledon all my life, that he could imagine . . . She handed him the tux in front of the church. He had a bit of a Christian upbringing. And she was getting him dressed, and he was almost having a good time. People kept stopping, and he loved new shirts. There was joking, just like in a locker room, a few of his buddies came. And friends won't hurt a friend, only when they have to, only when she's beautiful. They laughed. That in our country only every other couple gets divorced. After that, they only joked about the final exam. She almost didn't need to be there any more. He really didn't even want to touch her. Really, he didn't want to touch her only because she liked him so much. Like he was used to . . . Since she was already naked. She got naked awfully fast. He wasn't bad, just spoiled . . . She didn't get to meet his parents, they didn't come.

She was still teary eyed. She hadn't yet recovered from the in health or for poorer, until death do you part, so she said, this is my husband. To two neighbours she had invited. But he didn't turn around, he was yapping with his buddies. From then on she said Paťo, like he was used to . . . And the whole time she had her hand on her heart. That was when she felt it for the first time. Because he got scared. He looked like a young boy who had tipped over, broken, smashed something. You're . . . little?? You were still little?? On the spot he couldn't come up with a way to say it among friends. There was no way . . . And then from beneath the T-shirt . . . she didn't want to bother him with pimples, two big ones and a million small ones . . . or hold him up, since he had said he was in a hurry, she heard him . . . how was I supposed to know that you're like in the old days. Good thing he didn't say like before the revolution . . . She poked her head out, he was pale, he hated blood. That's why he didn't play hockey. That's why he didn't play anything seriously . . .

Walks! Indispensable because of the baby. But there are people everywhere, even in the forest . . . All three of them only took two, and already after the first one she told herself, never again. They didn't do him any good, they made him feel bad, both of them were embarrassed. About the same thing, about her. The difference was that she was used to it . . . Otherwise he would have loved them. The looks, the shop windows. They made things bright, they cheered him up. Handbag in hand, he'd saunter down the street, with good posture, without a care. But now he was sucking his tooth in a funny way. How could he have been so excited with her, how could he have thrown caution to the wind, people could have been thinking. That bothered him more than anything. Not so much the stroller, but with such a wretch . . . It made no sense to him. He still didn't understand it. How did those crazy seconds happen? It wasn't even dark there. She just whispered, turn out the lights. What for, he thought, I've already seen you. What went through his mind was how obedient she was, and then the wave rolled in. After it crashed, he gasped, he had to catch his breath, because he had forgotten to inhale. Because he didn't feel her. Did he have his back to her?! He didn't even hear her. No one moaned. Only afterwards she meowed like a little kitten . . . a little girl.

They only left the apartment together two or three times. He always caught himself at the last minute, I should have already been there, I'm off, I blew it again, I'm off, and he darted down the stairs. And it took her a quarter of an hour with the whole kit and kaboodle, her purse in her teeth. Literally . . . Even when they went on those two walks, he had gone ahead to check on the stroller. And Pipina, her teeth full as usual, carried down the baby, the bags, and the trash. For one, she didn't want to make two trips, and for another, where would she have left the baby, upstairs or downstairs . . . He didn't even bother pulling the teabag out of his tea. What for! She started to leave hers in too. But she still took out his spoon. He had hazelnut-golden eyes . . . Nearsighted, as it turned out. One time he dropped his contact, and it landed in the drain. Pipina froze. It was strange to hear foul language at home. Men's language . . . And what went through her head was, how was she going to teach the baby to say pardon me, when he kept saying what?

13

One time she really got a fright. She was bathing the baby, that is, she was about to bathe the baby, and he walked in. She turned around with the showerhead in her hand and sprayed him. With warm water. For a second she felt like she had shot him. He went all soft, limp, his eyes popped out of their sockets in astonishment, time stopped . . . Only once he had to take a breath did time move again. It was slowly getting going, and he, as if in zero gravity, clumsily shaking the droplets from his sweater, from his hands, shaking his head in disbelief, he backed out of the bathroom. Sorry! Don't . . . And he was quiet the rest of the evening. And when, after a long time, she laughed a little, he looked deep into her eyes, he hadn't forgiven her . . . What if it reminded him of something terrible, something from his childhood, she was very upset, she kept guilting herself about it . . . It would take me half a day, he'd say when people on TV were going down unimaginable hills at 60 miles per hour. I think I'll have a heart attack, when someone was struggling. He never said, hats off . . . Oh, everyone's like that, takes one to know one, she thought happily . . . And he slurped like a pig. Like a piglet, she corrected herself . . . And he farted and expectorated. And I don't?? Secretly to boot . . .

He had already taken his racquets too. And she couldn't imagine why he'd come by there again. Hardly because of the baby. He kept a respectful six-foot distance from it . . . She doubled over. She had a knot in her stomach, it was fear. Of all the things that needed to be done, taken care of, thought through, secured, not forgotten, not mistaken, dared. Terror, that she didn't know anything. Physics, geography. Even my ice skating's pitiful. And I've never done a headfirst dive either. My awful mother kept giving me spelling tests, a lot of good that did . . . She lost several nights' sleep because everything cost something. A scooter, dice, cookies. Maybe

14

I'll lose weight. But it was absurd to joke . . . Still, it's hard to believe that people get to take babies home from the hospital. Even people who've never done anything like it, never tried it or studied it. And they get sent home with them, the most precious . . .

When she fell asleep, she dreamed about a bush. It looked like a small sun. The closer Pipina got to it, the more it fluttered and shimmered. She squinted and reached out to see if it gave off heat too, then she backed away. She had almost touched a wasp! The bush was full of small yellow flowers, and bees and wasps that looked just like the flowers! On every flower buzzed two or three angry beasties . . . And the baby whimpered, and Pipina woke up. Because beware, the cat must take care!

She called herself Pipi . . . Her mommy used to call her that. But more and more often she called herself Pipina. Whenever she forgot, screwed up, mixed up, didn't do something on time, didn't know, didn't find something. She had an awful lot of didn'ts in her repertoire. On her tab . . . Just that night! She turned the water on for the baby's bath. She tested it, it was pleasant as could be, she even said to the baby, oh-so-pleasant, you will see. But the baby, who had been looking forward to it, kept frowning more and more, until she finally figured it out, until it finally dawned on her, that the water kept getting warmer. And before the stupid cow reacted, because as always, she didn't have enough hands, the baby was screaming bloody murder. My God, Pipina, you're such a stupid cow, resounded through the apartment from morning 'til night. From the difficult morning until the merciful night . . . But you've got to live. And for two! And cheerfully and with love! Because that's what the baby needs most, cheerfully, and with love, and for two. And one of them should be a man like a mountain.

Who knows everything and has the energy for it all. And who can reach! The way she did on a chair with a small stool on top of it . . . On a regular basis she was so tired that the whole day she looked forward to sitting, just getting to sit on the steps in front of their door, once the baby was finally asleep. They lived on the top floor, no one went up there. That position, those steps, they made her feel good. Those edges pressed into her achy back just right. That grey darkness was just right for a grey, overworked dust rag. Finally she could be who she was. Drooping, forgotten, fallen out of the window. She froze . . . She got so scared that shivers ran down her whole body. Who knows how many hundreds of her neurons died. I can't die. It's very important, it's the most important thing. I can't die, because beware, the cat must take care. And quicklyquickly she tried not to imagine how the baby would whimper as a test, as if it had gotten frightened . . . and then, thankgoodness, the gate clicked. A wonderfully worn gate. Imagination is a great servant, but a cruel master. And someone was going home uphill and didn't bother turning on the lights. He was already one floor below her, and a little star flew across the hallway, and it reeked. The door under Pipina's butt opened and closed, and Pipina almost exploded from anger. Once again, while struggling down the stairs with everything tomorrow, she'd have to bend over with the lot of it, pick up that cigarette butt, find a sewer . . . heeelp, she whimpered. Quietly, so no one would hear her.

And sometimes she dreamed about plants. Giant shrubs, almost trees with huge flowers in a disgusting green and yellow colour. With purple veins. Like varicose veins. They must have been the size of a head . . . But Pipina never saw one in bloom. She couldn't catch one blooming! Not a single one . . . There were buds, and then ditto, just spent, fallen to the ground. Nowhere a flower in

16

its prime! Only buds and corpses. Straaange . . . Pipina hated that dream. They didn't bloom, they just died and fell off. And then they lay on the ground like rags. They rotted and stank. She had that dream quite often . . .

What she feared most was when the baby would notice. When it would notice that there were too few of them. That there weren't enough of them . . . And the baby would ask. Why does everyone else have and I don't? And then the other children would ask. When who knows where comes only . . . and so ugly to boot. My mommy's a hundred times prettier, and my mom's a bajillion times prettier. And I've got a daddy and you don't! You're an idiot! You're alone . . . And my pop has a girlfriend at work with tits the size of soccer balls. She actually made me coffee with cognac. Piss off . . . And then it's here. Puberty . . . Puberty's no picnic. Puberty is like the word itself. Odd, dangerous, a little vulgar. Puberty's a terror, Pipina's terrible mother used to say . . . But as Dust Rag, that is, Pipina listened to the house . . . as she listened to how everyone around her struggled, sometimes more, sometimes less, how they meandered . . . she too became less scared of the darkness ahead. From a burned-out electrical outlet, to abandoned cancer. And she only wished . . . Whenever they walked by a church, under a big tree, in the setting sun, anywhere dignified, where he could be, if he happened to exist . . . for the baby to love her . . . But when the baby fixed its eyes on her, those eyes that didn't blink so as not to miss anything . . . she got really nervous, whether she was good enough. Because the baby didn't have a choice. It couldn't have had a choice if I'm its mother . . . But more than anything, she didn't want to bother the baby someday, annoy it, since she had no one else . . . that was what she wished for from Santa. You don't have to bring me anything else.

Good thing she was used to it. Because an ugly person is alone most of the time. Alone with herself. And at the same time, she doesn't like herself. At times, she hates herself . . . So tomorrow at school she'll have bloody scratches again. She'll put a Band-Aid on it, and everyone will laugh. Actually, they'll just have a quick laugh. Only at first glance. There won't be a second one, they'll have forgotten, lost interest . . . The fact that she's blushing doesn't cross anyone's mind, she's had problematic skin since first grade. Only the teachers see her any more. And it's clear to them how much she's suffering, how much she's struggling, the poor thing. She's a poor thing, that's obvious. And it makes them uncomfortable. At work. The educators . . . So they prefer to look elsewhere, they only call on her when absolutely necessary, at least if she studied . . . They already know what she's starting to suspect, but can't yet imagine. Loneliness of the no-one-needs-me kind is more monstrous than loneliness of the no-one-likes-me kind. It's all consuming. Corrosive. It ends with the murder of John Lennon, or the dead behind a girl who sat down in the middle of the road with her back to oncoming traffic . . . And we will forever miss Lennon's songs and his cheekiness, because they're exactly what we need, but can't do, and we will always pause over the innocent victims of a large collision, but the names of those who had caused it, the ones responsible, we'll forget immediately. In one ear, out the other. That was precisely why they did it . . . But all they managed to do was spread the injustice, they didn't take off theirs. Because you can't take off your skin, as you well know. Because already in preschool little people are dressed in pretty or ugly clothes, in pretty or ugly skin. If you have ugly skin and ugly clothes, already in preschool no one will say bye-bye to you . . . If you're a pale unsightly nothing, or a fat red nil in the corner . . . and everyone takes all your things, and on top of it they shove you . . . for no reason at all, just to try it . . . and you, instead of trying to come up with what might help, karate, or ballet, start to fret . . . your breasts will never grow big, nor will you wee high up a tree, it's done, it's over . . . And it's worse for girls, because a man can be uglier than sin, and a boy a thousand times more so, yet they still get to criticize! The long and the short of it is that we'll always feel sorry for Lennon, and not give a damn about them. And they belong in jail! It's only us ugly ones who know that maybe they're glad to belong anywhere at all. To have a place. Like pebbles in a pond. A merciful one. It doesn't reflect . . . But in jail that's a problem!

The world of the ugly is ruled by injustice. Because there is no justice when there are beautiful and ugly girls in the world. And the majority in the middle. The middling majority. And just to be on the safe side, they grab one another by the hands, feet, all things middle, and they become the audience for the glamour girls and the gorgeous guys. And caustic critics of the ugly. Everyone likes less-crooked legs, a less-flat butt. They couldn't possibly be kind, even though they know a thing or two about what it's like to have teeth like a rabbit, to laugh with their gums . . . For the first who-knows-how-many years nothing else actually matters. Lookin' good, as someone from Bratislava would say, or averted eyes. Looking elsewhere. Your own look away wherever you're reflected. You choose not to believe your own eyes, and you watch whether others look the same in the mirror as they do in reality. They do, no light will fix it! Neither the light nor the viewing angle is to blame. The blame is on your dad. And it can't be fixed with a makeup pad . . . Only once the glamour girls start to turn grey and fade away, it turns out that you may know something. That you're not a friend disguised as a swine, that you cook well, that you don't speak out of your ass, or say the same things all the time, your punctuality's nice too . . . A beauty can show up to a date late, or not at all. Does it matter? No! Only when she starts to turn grey and fade away does it become a problem. Annoying enough to kill her!

And the glamour girls and the gorgeous guys didn't just stock up on confidence. They also figured out jokes and humour . . . Because even when they flopped a few times, no one rolled their eyes, and they tried again. At least some practical, light joking around. And now it's in their life basket. Not as a talent, not as a life philosophy, just as trick number G7. So they joke around, their teeth gleam, and no one cares that it's their second, make that third, set. And then the people . . . who are supposed to make our lives easier, not harder, for example a sales clerk or a civil servant, bend over backwards to do only for them what is their doggone duty, what they get paid for . . . Oh, and some noncommittal, light flirting comes in handy too. To remind the other person that he is of the opposite sex and I know it, I can feel it, or as the case may be, that it's still visible. And she ran into men, women . . . the before was hard to imagine any more, but they must have been bitchin', because they were still so full of themselves. Like their butts in jeans a long time ago. They had barely noticed socialism . . . And after the revolution, they instantly set themselves up with millions to start, because they were in the right place at the right time. Because they didn't just look good, they were also clever . . . But where are the ugly ones supposed to pick up the civil servant trick? They blew every joke, because the lack of interest made them choke up. Speaking at all had taken incredible effort, blazing courage, but no one was listening. So the little voice broke, and they were embarrassed until four in the morning. They rolled around in bed because they had missed the punch line. And then they fell asleep, and they were late. They slipped into the classroom like worthless shadows, the others were already writing. Only two girls lifted their mascara-laden eyelashes, but they didn't even nudge anyone. Yeah, Pipina was used to it . . . Bumping up the stairs with the stroller by herself. Once again, no one sees me! The woman, who needs someone to pitch in, but she is like sin. And what made her most unhappy . . . was that she only thought bad things. That she was like sin on the inside as well as on the outside.

Her apartment was really getting her down. A poor old panel-construction apartment, chilled to the bone. Ice-cold hands and feet were in fashion there spring and fall. In the winter, three pairs of warm socks, in the summer, swelter! Everything opened, including the door to the hallway. Exhaust from the street everywhere, the stench of gasoline everywhere . . . Only the curtains had it good all year. Playing around all year, cuddling. The wind blew through the cracks around the windows . . . She was almost afraid of her apartment, it was unpredictable. Whenever she turned on the washing machine, ironed, and needed to cook at the same time, she had to reset the main breaker in the hallway. So the baby ended up going to sleep when it was almost time for it to get up. So nothing terrible happened, she just realized that anytime she could . . . The poor outlets had been stinking for a long time. The one by the stove had blown right in front of her disbelieving eyes. Now there was an extension cord running through the whole kitchen to the stove. Before the baby can walk, something should be done about that . . . Whenever she was coming home, she stealthily watched people from the bus stop onward, to see if they were behaving as usual, if they weren't turning to look at her. And when she turned down their street, she always shot a glance upwards, to see whether there wasn't a glow, and as she got closer, she looked for charring around the windows. What if it's already over, and the tired firefighters have already wiped the well-earned sweat and soot off their brows and scooted off. She saw them the way I see you. Imagination is a great servant, but . . . Even the plumbing fixtures were pitiful. If you stopped, you could hear dripping. Just like during a thaw, when it's spring. From every direction . . . She knew how to fix a leaking toilet, and she had to do it often. She even had her mother's washing machine, it reminded her terribly of her terrible mother . . . And anyone could kick down the front door. In an instant she could imagine everything, including the unimaginable shadow over her. So she put the meat cleaver that had never been used under her bed. Before the baby can walk, something should be done about that . . . And the only way anyone could get into her kitchen was over her dead body! For years no one had been in it, except Paťo and one neighbour. Who had forced her way in and then backed out, amused, her wide eyes jumping around like little birds. No doubt she had told everyone about it, described it in detail, that pitiful, fully primordial state of the kitchen, worn to the core, with concrete showing through the linoleum. Pipina was so embarrassed . . . The baby still took naps in the mornings and in the afternoons, but someone was always fixing something, sawing, drilling, and the baby was restless, and Pipina squirmed and kept hanging things all over the place, and using every pillow as a sound barrier . . .

Someone called the fire department. But there was no need just yet. So when the aerial platform was floating by the house with a young man like the virgin . . . Pipina opened her window and said, just a moment. And the fireman didn't even have time to be surprised, she was already handing him a fragrant cup of coffee. That dashing man smiled, completely disarmed, and said, I'll be coming back . . . That tiny cup on a little plate floated three stories above the street, on the most beautiful tray possible, on the palm of his hand. And Pipina beat her head against the pillow until morning, to stop dreaming about Paťo . . .

And the apartment building started to be afraid, it kept getting locked. I wouldn't touch that with a ten-foot pole, boys chatted about not-so-good-looking girls on a bench under the windows, which had seen its share of action. But one of the girls was a good student, and one of the boys wasn't. In a nutshell, he needed her, to a point, he said, and the bench moaned, it was an experienced bench . . . But that good student must not have done exactly what the boy wanted, when he wanted, how he wanted . . . and this non-soundproof apartment building had never heard such an outburst of the most vulgar words with unprecedented, unheard of adjectives. Neither in volume nor in obscenity. Nor had it ever been shaken by such loud banging of every door he came across . . . But outside, under the windows, out in fresh air . . . the fucking sweaty cunt turned into, God knows why . . . we C-students will never understand the mental U-turn of an F-student . . . you know, Simi, I had to get it out of my system. Blow off some steam, he said. And the apartment building was terrified, what if Simonka loves him! If that's the case, she should be buried right now, get it over with as soon as possible. It would be better for the apartment building too . . . Who knows how many little kids had heard that. How it had dropped into their bowed little heads, like into piggy banks . . .

And Pipina had a nice dream and she remembered it. She was walking along a riverbank. A riverbank? A riverbank. In a long arc. And she saw a couple from a distance. Almost from when they were dots. The wind carried over their laughter, and the dots grew bigger and prettier, until he was more beautiful than she. By then it wasn't polite to stare, otherwise Pipina would have been all eyes . . . She just glanced over a few times, pretending to blink, the woman had hair like sand. Heavy like that too . . . And with her head completely bowed, Pipina only saw their hands and feet. Bare feet. And an old word came to her mind, noble. Then the young man said hello to her . . . Pipina bowed her head deeper to say thank you, and she felt like she had been given something . . . And when she thought about it in the morning, it was like looking at a gift again . . .

In the morning the baby kept whimpering and wanted to be in her arms the whole time. And there was no hot water, and then the power went out. She soothed the baby and said shhh, shhh, to the both of them. I can't even do the basic things, the baby's hard-won schedule will be blown, it'll get sick . . . I won't be able to wash my hair, and my mother-in-law is coming this evening. Banging on the door. She froze. Right, there's no electricity. And she felt completely deflated, she's here. The place is a wreck . . . Why do people never do what they say, she asked herself on her way to the door. The door almost hit her as her mother-in-law barged in. What do you caaare when I come ooover, you don't dooo anything all day. Her mother-in-law sniffed every corner and turned towards Pipina, almost retching. The least you could dooo is brush your haaair. Nothing got past her . . . I think the baby's getting sick, she whispered through her unbrushed teeth. Paťko was neeever sick. He had a rigid scheeedule, if you know what that iiis. Pipina took a breath. Well, I've seen you twooo, I'm oooff. I don't haaave time to waste, like your mooother. It was all Pipina could do not to cover her ears. You poor unheaaalthy thing. You liiittle neglected, unhaaappy mite. Before leaving, the mother-in-law tickled the baby's belly, and the baby seemed to like it . . . And so Pipina didn't stick to even the most basic schedule, and when the baby dozed off like a little log, like a healthy little rock, the mother-in-law must have cured it, Pipina also stretched out. And she had a dream . . . god knows why, about an outdoor cinema! The screen was still down over the water. Over a bay! It started going up, and behind it glimmered the other side of the bay. And a city! It was impossible to tell the city lights from their reflections in the water. In places where nothing shimmered, giant dark trees jutted out, or their shadows sprawled . . . And in front of the screen . . . in the whispers of the waves, leaves, and lovers' dialogues, flew bats. Dozens of them . . . Everything was black and white. The movie as well as the dream . . .

And the day went on. They took a tram to the housing administration office, something needed to be done about that apartment! And they were standing over two young men, who had barely managed to fold themselves up like ladders into the tram seats. Elbows protruding everywhere, knees kneeing everything. Side by side with an older, plus-sized woman and her even older, even more plus-sized bags . . . I personally don't know a single kind person. Do you mean kind or caring? The tram's ears perked up. I mean a kind, caring person. There's a difference, a person who's caring is not necessarily kind. No, that's not right, a person who's caring is automatically kind. No, that's not right, a person who's

25

kind doesn't have to be caring at all. You can be caring towards someone, but kind to everyone. Or it's the other way around, you can be caring to all, but kind only to some . . . But Pipina never found out which way it really works, because she was helping the woman with the big bags and even bigger varicose veins off the tram. She had seen them up close, because first the woman had helped Pipina with the stroller. And as they were getting off in stages, the tram wanted to shut its doors, and they kept yelling for help. Then the woman said . . . please, don't be mad at me, today's the worst day of my life . . . Who knows what conclusion those two guys, large of body and soul, had reached, but the fact that Pipina had peed her panties a tiny bit was certain. Those bags were heavier than the stroller . . . In the end she was glad that the housing administration office was closed that day. To be exact, it had been open, but the opening hours were over. By five minutes. And everything was quiet, spotless. All cleaned up. Not a peep . . . The receptionist did say, this is no zoo, miss!

And she was standing in the sea . . . A light offshore breeze on her face. And on the beach in front of her, seagulls, one right next to another. Like piano keys. With their backs to Pipina . . . Other than that, not a soul around, let alone a small tree or a bit of shade to squat down in. Pipina really needed to pee, and those seagulls could have turned around at any moment. So she peed in the sea. It was warm and smelled like balm. It was glad. To make a long story short, she peed herself . . . And in the morning she asked the baby whether it also dreamed when it went. The baby just looked at her, but didn't tell. Perhaps when they're better friends, give it some time. But I can't go around peeing myself! Though there's nothing more pleasant than peeing into the fragrant, warm sea . . .

One time he was home in the afternoon . . . And the baby was sleeping. It was that well-deserved free hour and a half for adults. He was reading the paper, and she was ironing baby clothes. And she pretended it was the only thing this adult hour and a half together could be spent on. After the wedding they made love three times. Altogether, four times . . . Now a strange wind was blowing, and the old window started to rattle, it was warped. It banged harder and harder, and she waited as long as she could, she must have wanted to wake up the man in him, the technician, the home repairman, but at some point she couldn't take it any more. May I, you've already read the first page, may I, you don't need the first page any more, do you? Huh . . . And Pipina folded that title page into a thick wad, pressed it into the gap on the side of the window, and there was silence . . . It was quiet as the grave, until, from behind the paper came, these socialist buildings are such crap . . . No mention of getting an apartment together. He was still living with his mommy. A Bratislava native through and through.

One day the house was like a jukebox. It resonated gently like a hive. The man on the ground floor wasn't screaming, and on the first floor a piano was playing. A simple tune, therefore, no mistakes. She meowed like a kitten. She produced a meow like a content little kitten. It used to drive her mommy crazy . . . And whenever she lifted something heavy and groaned, that too upset her mother. Do you want someone to hear you . . . And if she licked her fingers while eating, that also bothered her mother. They're looking . . . It wasn't until recently that Pipina had figured out it was reminiscent of sex. Probably! It wasn't until recently that Pipina had put two and two together, that her awful mother had been leading by example. Probably . . . She had never seen her flirt, show off. Even though it's actually strange to talk to men the same way as to women. It wasn't until recently that Pipina had realized that her mother had been steering her. Because she knew, because she saw. Probably . . . Girls are always thinking and talking about what they'll wear the next day. And they pray for good weather, so that they can. New sandals, you know. High heels, you know. To the pool, you know. They had pre-tanned somewhere under a window. They're looking, you know. You know that they're looking . . . And by the end of the summer, most of them prayed that only one be looking. He totally stayed, he didn't leave, you know. Until dark, you know . . . You didn't leave either. Afterwards I left. But don't tell anyone, OK . . . Pipina, on the other hand, would spend the whole evening crying because she had reached the conclusion that tighter jeans couldn't take off extra pounds. Not only did you have to plan an extra ten minutes in the morning for it, but everything got smeared all over as well. And the seams cut into your skin and produced more and more juices with every step. So then you smelled like a . . . A friend of hers had told her she stank like that. Out of nowhere, when they were talking about who wanted a cat. At least five girls had heard it . . . Her mother couldn't have cared less about what she wore. As long as it wasn't dirty and it didn't have holes. And as long as you weren't cold, that was the most important thing. But maybe she was just steering Pipina, because she knew, because she saw. Probably. Because she was a mother . . . But then she just died. Then she just up and died, and that was that . . . And she left Pipina, day and night, no help in sight, amen . . .

And Pipina dreamed that they met her mother at a crosswalk. At her crosswalk, no less! On the most direct path from the door of her building to the door of the store. And vice versa. What about the fact that the path crossed two sets of tram tracks and two two-lane roads? I've got eyes, don't I? And they can see me, can't they . . . Mom, it's dangerous! What's dangerous is that filthy, dark underpass with those slippery steps that crumble like Tatra mountain paths! She was right, as usual . . . So her mother was standing on the sidewalk in front of the store, smiling. Pipina hadn't seen that smile in years. What a beautiful baby, she said . . .

Beauty and ugliness are forever. Even if they don't last. That boy who liked you in your sophomore year in high school, he became a doctor. And he's pleased to see you when he spots you in the waiting room full of whining and sneezing. You remind him of something better than this place, besieged since god's morning by angry, worried women. For example, that he wanted to be an astronaut! He told you about it because he wanted to sound interesting. Because you had the longest hair in the class . . . But what goes through his mind, because he's already in a better mood, is, I may have been dead by now. But famous . . . Still, he's glad to see you on this chilly, snotty morning, when everyone's hacking. In fact, he's glad in general. Because viewed through the lens of the declining options of the reality of adulthood, a doctor is more than enough. Currently, he's omnipotent. And you see it! He could have whichever woman he wants, and you know it, but he calls you . . . And a wave of bliss washes over you. As a woman, but also because you got the baby out of the sea of germs. In the waiting room you didn't even set the baby down, you had the feeling that the lower you went, the denser it got. That filth is like an anvil

29

plus gravity! You take as shallow of breaths as possible. But you can't explain that to the baby. That you had managed this monstrous, screaming to high heaven injustice because the doctor had once laid his head on the desk behind you and covered himself with your hair. And it was freshly washed! Because beauties wash their hair every day. In order to be beauties! And he'll be looking for that fragrance forever. Even once he doesn't know why any more . . . But how are you to save your baby from the sea of germs if you have a few perma-oily tufts of hair tortured to death by back-combing? Children shouldn't suffer because of their parents, but they do . . .

Pipina prayed. For the light to turn green! As always, at this, the smoggiest of intersections. She looked and she couldn't believe her eyes. A woman was walking around on the opposite sidewalk. Back and forth. Slowly enough so that a little girl who was obviously happy to be able to walk could keep up. Holding a hand she was doing pretty well . . . And that cow was looking at storefronts, while the excited little girl inhaled lungsful of exhaust. Her little head was roughly at the level of the tailpipes that could cross the desert or go up a hill, but instead they were there. And they were bored and spewing poisons . . . Little people shouldn't pay the price for big people, but they do. Specifically, with cancer when they grow up . . .

No one remembers an ugly young woman. No one's proud that the whole town's still talking about how they walked down Main Street. Fabulous. Holding hands. And they knew that everyone was watching them hold hands. That it was a big deal . . . And the fountain still remembers how he sat on it afterwards, because a fountain remembers everything. He was fabulous, but sad. And she was walking down Main Street with some other lucky guy. It wasn't such a big deal any more, such a together forever, it was just by the pinkies, but everyone was watching, what does he think about it? Nothing. Clenched jaws. But with class . . . Except that now . . . now everyone is us. Even the rivals! And it's all our fabulous times. Our all-important, all-bragging-worthy times! What you had on . . . What you were wearing was more important than health and snow and frost all put together. And some jeans you'd kill for, and others you wouldn't put on even if they killed you. And a pair of legs in a mini was the Holy Grail. They could go wherever they wanted to, and everyone was defenceless. And the legs turned towards music school, and the others had to deal with it elsewhere. The grail was still only kissing on the cheek . . . But once in a while that young thing realized she had struck something. A heart. One day a boy's, another day a jealous girl's. They remembered it forever, she had a hazy recollection . . . And then things got more and more serious . . . until the only thing that mattered was who with who . . . and the grail started to lie too, that it was at a piano lesson . . . but only from the waist down . . . You know, he stole Jola from me, but then she dumped him and dated Ico. In the end she married Edo. And I dumped Mima, and in the end she married Ico. In America. And Jola was naked with me once, but Edo came back. First from Argentina, then to Jola, and then both of them off to the hills. And they're there to this day, painters . . . And we're all one big family and we remember everything. Including the fact that no one remembers you!

And then we're all getting divorced. Perla and Miki! We're really sad about that, they were the first, respected. They were really sleeping together. Like adults. Even the teachers knew about it . . . And all of us have nicknames and diminutives. Forever. Even in advanced middle age of middling people that adulthood has beaten us into . . . we wave to each other from sidewalk to sidewalk, hi Softie, hey Smash!! And for half an hour the braggart's swagger's back, feeling the dagger . . . in an evening town panting for a summer day . . . Not even in old age will we all be equal. Even when the only thing left to compete over is who will last longer, we'll only keep up with our own. Not even a dog will bark after some poor flat-chested girl that no one had groped on the sly!

Miki, for the most private moments! That was her slogan. Miki was the one she had swiped, stolen for herself. Whose coat she secretly smelled in the coatroom at school. From the inside. She took a good look around and dove in. She immersed herself in it. It was cold in there, strange . . . When she surfaced, she looked guilty like a tiny bug whose rock had been lifted. And his amazing coat hung by the sleeve, busted . . . The next day she brought a needle and thread, and looking around, terrified, she wouldn't have been able to explain this, she sewed on the torn loop. Then she pinned the needle to the inside of her pocket and wound the thread around it. That way, whenever she wanted, she could touch the thing that had touched the thing that had touched him . . . Miki . . . She wasn't even jealous. She didn't believe she was the only one who had him for her most private moments. And one time, when she had the best one ever, she thought that maybe he could have felt it. That at least the last ripples could have reached him. The way someone could sense that someone else had died . . . And she thought about how good he must have had it since he was so perfect, so good looking. She was happy for him. One time she said to him, hi Miki, not just hi, as usual. He never answered, he must not have heard, her throat was always awfully tight . . . Hi Miki, burst out of her unexpectedly, because he had unexpectedly crossed her path. He must not have heard again, but then he turned around, looked at her, and turned back. A beautiful face of stone, a back as tall as a wall. And then she heard it, then he said hi . . . And then he let her last name slip. By now he may be president . . .

What's young is good does not apply among the young. How do girls treat their ugly classmates? The smart ones treat them like invalids, the dumb ones treat them as inferior . . . But none of them understand that we want pretty dresses too. What for?? It's like when fat people eat, what for?? And if an ugly girl is a good student? So what?? What else could she be doing?? Ugly girls don't think about anything other than being ugly, pretty girls only think about being pretty. And whether they're pretty enough. And what looks good on them. Ugly girls keep looking around as if they were in the jungle, pretty girls don't see anything but themselves. One time she wanted to kill herself, by then her awful mother had ditched her, she had already died, but then it crossed her mind that they'd see her naked. And she had heard that people sometimes poop themselves. So she kept suffering. Hair over the disgusting fat cheeks, hands flailing around to cover the awful teeth. The body either in something like a tent or skintight. For the life of her she couldn't decide which one made her look less fat. At night she wrote painful reflections about life, and in the morning she couldn't read them. Youth is hell.

No one had ever taught Pipina how to ski well. Because that's what boyfriends are for. She had only been on skis on two school trips, but there too the people teaching, having a good time, were boyfriends. So the ugly girls struggled at the very end of the line. With wet knees, wet butts, broken nails, in tears. From the wind! And they were terribly embarrassed when the kids in high spirits, hot from exertion, without hats, had to wait for them . . . When they finally emerged from around the bend, the ones who were always first took off impatiently, they had waited! But when were the ones who were always last supposed to rest . . . Not at night. Because all the kids who liked one another were having a good time downstairs, and all the ones who weren't liked were upstairs, agonizing over the fact that no one missed them. In tears. Without wind. Regardless of gender.

And tomorrow the sun will rise again, and the tide always brings in something. Pipina was struggling to get up off the stairs, and her hands paused at the small hillocks of her breasts. With tiny nipples, even though she was nursing. She caressed them. They were warm, soft, good, productive, her mammary glands had nothing to be ashamed of. The baby loved them and sucked on them every which way. It had a refined technique . . . She went in. She should be reading something, soon the baby will start asking questions, why . . . She didn't watch TV, it was full of beautiful people. Worldly people. They looked so good they could have been mistaken for one another. So one woman had dark hair, one was a blonde, and another was a redhead. A few accompanied by the opposite sex. Mostly. And the redhead was with someone in a wheelchair. Though otherwise unattainable. He had been steeled by suffering. Now he could give advice about it! Out of the corner of his mouth. Dubbed all too well, she didn't understand a word . . . Only rarely did someone not look good, but then he was as bad as the devil. The trade-off was that he was easy to understand . . . If she did watch, she watched the extras. She watched the average people that were used to being the extras for the glamour girls and the gorgeous guys. She watched who was trying to stick out, and how hard they were working. What if . . . And she liked to watch how nervous actors became when faced with danger. From animals or children. Who weren't going where they were supposed to, that barked when they weren't supposed to. Who cried and looked elsewhere, not at them! She paid the closest attention to small babies. Whether their heads were being properly supported! And she always remembered which moron didn't! Good looking, but a moron! And when an actress didn't pay attention to that, she had no words for it. Cow Cowski! One time she saw an actress bottle feed a baby, but the formula was below the level of the nipple! Because the only thing the woman cared about was what she looked like! How pitiful . . . And she always had tears in her eyes when a baby was reaching for its mother, somewhere beyond the camera. And if it wasn't reaching, she grumbled. They must have bought it on the cheap in some orphanage! The most important thing was not to make sharp movements with them, quick transfers from person to person. A different smell, different wrinkles, different heartbeat, a different nose up close, from below, and then another completely different perfume! A disgusting one . . . For a brief period of time, she watched the news while nursing. But when the first guy, the one she trusted because he looked unassuming and kind, and had a deep voice, and once in a while he rambled on fabulously, because he never read anything off a piece of paper . . . one week he said that he stood behind what he had said . . . the next week he was gone, and the third week he showed up somewhere else . . . she simply lost interest. Public matters.

There was only one thing she watched. The one about how they were all together so beautifully. In beautiful nature. And it was beautifully warm there. And big trees, and serious work. And flies. And most of all, the beautiful Southern Cross . . . And most of all, everyone loved someone. Like it was meant to be. Granted, over time every one had loved everyone, but that took a while, they were honest people. Truthful. If someone lied, he was done for. For at least ten episodes. It dragged on beautifully . . . The best part was when one of them really liked another, when they desired one another, the actors! When their hands wandered where they weren't supposed to, where it wasn't polite, where the breasts began! When their ears turned red. Hers did too! And they kissed after a brief, real hesitation, a flash of understanding, and their lips didn't stick. That was her strongest memory . . . Oh, how she wanted Paťo . . . She planned her whole day, her whole week, so that she could watch them. They were her family. Saturday, Sunday were clear. And they kept missing one another, and coming back, and overcoming obstacles, and in the end they understood. With their hearts. But they all helped each other. In the everyday, difficult battle with life . . . They never rambled, and every third sentence was a punchline. And the best actors, the ones she liked most, were funny. They were supposed to be funny, and sometimes it even came across in the translation. It was great . . . And then the actors would go to a good hotel, eat a great dinner together, and laugh and laugh. They'd only part ways briefly, only to take a shower. And the excited, overjoyed drops would flow down, run down to beautiful places and tickle . . . What went on after that, she couldn't quite imagine, the way we can't fully imagine paradise. And she couldn't remember the last time she laughed . . . And she envied anyone who belonged somewhere . . . To a group, a team, a couple, the same feeling. She felt terribly lonely. The baby didn't help, it was part of her. There was just a little more of her. And that was what she feared most. That she'd teach it nothing but sad things . . . Then there was the sound of sucking air. The breast was empty. And the baby was sleeping like a little angel . . .

The alarm went off. Jesus, I think it's Wednesday. Wednesday, we'll-need-him-before-it-ends-day. My God, there's no hot water. Jeepers, I'll hang myself. God, I can't even do that. Morning is the worst part of the day. Christ, what time is it? Ring . . . She got so startled that a million neurons smarted and died. Wednesday, mother-in-law. Ring . . . She jumped up, pulled off her shirt. Ring . . . She sat down on the bed. Ring . . . She stared under her feet. Ring . . . She got up. Ring . . . She put the shirt on, went to get the door. Ring, right in her face. You looook aw-great. What were you doooing at night. Please, come in . . . You ruined his life, so finish him oooff today. He's the one who filed for divorce. Can you blaaame him?? . . . Pipina was brushing her teeth, but it seemed rude to close the door. And she wanted the baby to see her first when it woke up. By the way, you have to set up baaabysitting a week in advaaance. The papers came the day before yesterday. It's a meeess in here. It's morning. It's aaalways morning to you. Pipina clenched her fists. He had a mistress. Which oooone doesn't?? . . . Her mother-in-law was already on the balcony, shaking her head as she kept lifting the roughly hung-up laundry with her fingernail. It can't possibly dryyy this way. It can't, but it has to . . . And then the mother-in-law said something kind. All marriages are aaawful. Why should yours be any diiifferent. Thank you. Don't be so dramaaatic . . . The baby hadn't woken up yet, and she had to go. I hope it'll forgive me. For this too . . .

That night she dreamed about office plants . . . They even grew where people got divorced, where they were getting divorced. She kept looking at them. Those large, five-fingered, hard, shiny leaves. Much bigger than a man's hand. Terribly dusty. Pipina, with her eyes lowered, had to resist drawing a little heart on one of them as she left a different way than he did. But in a dream . . . but now in her dream there was a pitcher sitting on almost every green hand. A white pitcher with thick, hard, velvet walls. On one side open all the way down. She brought her face closer, it was as fresh in there as by an open window. In the middle was a yellow piston, like a banana. This must be a very different land. They're obviously doing well here! She didn't dare kiss the piston.

Up and at 'em! All over again! The same as always. Pipina pried open her eyelids with her hands. Morning is the most hateful part of the whole hateful day. And we have to go to the doctor. He won't tell me anything . . . once again he won't tell me anything I don't tell him, but maybe I'll walk away feeling like he would have at least noticed some deadly disease . . . Why the baby doesn't sleep, he doesn't know, but you must be doing something wrong, mom, otherwise the baby would sleep some. But the key is not to be glum, the baby needs a cheerful mom. Pipina started to worry that she wasn't cheerful enough, and that maybe it was why the baby wasn't sleeping . . . If only he knew that when things are a little better, when everything is more or less OK, I get bored. That's how awful a mom I am . . . Goodbye, I'm glad you've come, just work harder, mom . . . If I didn't have the baby that was slowly but surely killing me, I'd kill myself. Pipina bumped down the stairs with the stroller, the elevator wasn't working again. And no one helped her. No one saw her. Out of at least ten people in sight.

She woke up ten times a night. The chronically underslept lose the will to live. But they have lucid moments, because beware, the cat must take care. Because they're so vigilant, they're never quite asleep. And they're so tired, they can't tell whether they're awake or dreaming. She saw a beach . . . Teeming with women. Full of women. From the littlest to the biggest. All but the really little roly-polies. Starting with those that shriek like seagulls at the water's edge. And just like seagulls, they dip in their little toes, their little claws into the lace, and then they hop back out, giggling . . . And those who already have secrets sit around on benches. Best friends. The best students buttoned up to their chins. Not with dolls in their beds any more, but with plush toys smooched to baldness. Pebbles in secret hiding spots, diamonds for sure. Mom said they come in pink too . . . Where is my childhood, where has it gone . . . And then there are teenage girls of every variety. Some are still almost kids, still in a fog about how kids are made, others are practically actresses. In mysterious groupings. Groups running amok, and off somewhere, a lonely, offended shadow. All kinds of clubs. The one nearby is for studying makeup. Going back and forth between neighbouring purses. And next to them is the bench that won the which-can-fit-the-most contest. Occupied by the stretched-out-and-wrinkled. Everything five sizes too large, hair at least down to the waist, down past the butt is a dream, mouth full of barrettes. Only little girls save their snap clips! Secret talk about bras. What not to do, the thing to do is to have at least one strap showing! Barricaded bathrooms, first attempts at hair colouring. And terrible problems with the toilet. With all the toilets in the world. How to enter without being seen and leave even more inconspicuously. I'll buy anything, but toilet paper, no way. And then you need a gazillion times worse, pads, tampons. A tear glistens in mom's eye, a lifetime of suffering has begun. A strange connection with the universe continues incomprehensibly, the way it's supposed to . . . And not far off sticks out a big girl who's already like everyone's mom. Totally hunched over. She's embarrassed about too large too soon . . . Where is my girlhood, where has it all gone . . . And then there are two or three who already know what they have it for, and they've got serious problems. They can't possibly handle it. Madly in love with those who hurt them. Don't wake them up too soon . . .

And Pipina is either asleep or awake. And the wild flock is calming down. Only envy can manage something like that. One of them, already gorgeous, ripe for the picking, has her cell phone ring. She steps aside importantly, and just then a green cabriolet with two dark young men emerges from the setting sun. They couldn't be more handsome, if that's your cup of tea, and it certainly is this flock's! They want to squeal . . . But those two are only looking at her, at the heavenly one, the divine one. She's not looking at them, but a strand of her hair falls towards her mouth, onto her cell phone. The way it does about a hundred times an hour. The guys gulp . . . And she puts that dark, heavy snake about where it belongs. The way she does about a hundred times an hour. That dizzying cooperation of the long, transparent fingers, slightly open mouth, breasts that always sigh, that can't be learned, that's a talent . . . And the strand is back in her mouth, and she leaves it there and breathes with her cell phone. There isn't anyone in a hundred-foot radius not being consumed by envy or jealousy . . . And then she lifts two fingers about an inch in the direction of those two, and they get out, each in a single swift motion, and they fold the seats. She may enter whichever way she wants, whenever she wants, if she wants . . . And she, making out with her cell phone, gets in and sinks. The waterfall of hair is falling. She leans back, and it pours like a torrent. She snuggles up to the seat, and the hair becomes a dark lake. That can't be learned, that's a talent . . . And the front seats as well as the doors of the tiny two-door cabriolet, good only for showing off, drop into place . . . and the shiny, round, let's say lilac leaf, takes off into the setting . . . Who knows how it'll all end . . . What will slip through whose fingers . . .

And then the most important thing, marriage! And Pipina is either awake or asleep under a beach umbrella. My mother cried, mine too, mine too! And they shake their heads in amazement. I had a dress that I'll be able to use for an evening occasion. I rented a dress and almost spilled soup on it, I would have regretted that wedding. And I had a dress that covered . . . In the safe shadow of a few proud moms who had just given birth. It was—there are no words for it. Yet there have to be. Over and over again. In great detail . . . One shade over, the mothers who've already been through it. No doubt better than their mothers. You bet! Resolute, loud, practical, out for a well-deserved coffee. He's five months old, I'm not nursing any more! Three's plenty! You bet, I'm trying to lose weight . . . The ones who are nursing remain silent. They're fat . . . Almost all of them struggling financially, because it's high time to have everything. At least the hair not in a ponytail! I do everything in gloves, and the beautiful hands wander from a new hairdo to a cigarette. The ones who don't do anything in gloves remain silent. Their haircuts are also nothing to write home about . . . So far the only divorcee is the craziest girl in class. None are dead yet. Those who can pull off a low neckline, have it down to the waist. Those who can have their legs crossed, do so up to their panties. More than half are still wearing maternity clothes. On spread out bodies. It's not worth it yet . . . They may have been friends in difficult times, now there's no time. They barely managed to find a date to show off to their friends, to show their friends. They won't see each other for a long time, the hard work has begun . . . And all the things you don't know, you must learn. On the go, quickly! To be a great mother, wife, but especially housekeeper. Not just what you studied. When you were still foot-loose, when your mother did your ironing for you. She even clipped my toenails! And cut, and now it's your turn. Everything for everyone. From morning 'til night. And to be liked at night as well. And by your mother-in-law. And to do well at work. And to visit your mother at least once in a while. Not to be irritable. And your clock's ticking, so if you want a second one . . . so that the first one isn't alone, when we die . . . the suffocating responsibility is also new . . . And there's cooking to be done. At least in the even-ing. But don't eat in the evening. But meat! For your man . . . And men, that is, boys, don't have to do anything. Only what they studied. And they get a good night's sleep. They're not nursing. And you have to handle them like rotten eggs. So that they're enjoying themselves. Not having their feet up with their friends off somewhere at a basketball game. But that's still a secret. A mis-understanding. So there's the constant, my husband said, my husband thinks, my husband and I . . . And then he gets quiet, then he has a lot of work to do, then it's on the weekends too, and by then not even the kid-is-at-grandma's-and-a-new-hairdo will save it. And all of a sudden you're alone and blonde . . . You know, she wasn't giving me what I need any more! And were you?? No one asks that. And now there are a few young women with sad eyes even when they're laughing. What were you expecting, boys will be boys. But when we were classmates, we were all the same! Don't be ridiculous. And we wanted the same things. Don't be naive. But it worked for half of the class, just not for me . . . And over time it turns out there are fewer and fewer of them. Men from Mars, and all of them are married. And the children are growing up and not one of them studies. And you're embarrassed to talk about the things that didn't work out. And you know what, once was enough!

And Pipina is either awake or asleep. Out for coffee. With whipped cream, we only live once. But a cake, God forbid . . . Only God knows any more what they look like without dark glasses. Hats are good too. And the face needs to be protected, dressed. Too bad we didn't know about that before . . . They handle the everyday things with their hands tied behind their backs, anything outside of that, they have no patience for. Yesterday I kicked him out for good. Even that I had to do for him. He couldn't pluck up the courage to save his life. To pursue his happiness. He said he had been in love with her since they took dance lessons at school. Poor man . . . Mine's not going to have it easy, that young thing wants kids. Imagine doing it all over again. Poor man . . . I was supposed to babysit yesterday, but the other mother-in-law beat me to it . . . Mine send me pictures every now and then. I spend the whole evening crying . . . I have a great pill. Nonaddictive. Herbal. Good for your digestion, too. And you can take it with alcohol . . . It's just too fresh, this not being needed by anyone . . . A young man turns his head to look at them. He has a nagging feeling that they know something. That they have some kind of a trick for bliss. And they do. One of them. But she won't risk being vulnerable again.

And then the hats only look good on at most two. I'm old, not crazy! But little by little they all get excited again. You know, after all, those men are, simply put, gorgeous!! Those arms, that butt! That lil' Billy!! Grandmothers' crushes have the power of first loves. And they cook and they bake, as a matter of course. She gave what she had. Granddaughters don't know yet that it's not just about the cake . . . All those computers, you can put them . . . One old woman thinks where the sun don't shine, another, up . . . It would be difficult to find stronger personalities! But their granddaughters think that they know as little about everything as they do about computers. So they end up having to figure out everything on their own hides. Like those before them, and those before them. For example, whether it's better for your husband to cheat on you, or for him to die . . . Only some make it through one or the other. Only some won't have their mouths disappear from resentment. Only a few remain curious. Have the need to go everywhere. When there's music, dance. On the banks of the Danube. With Jozef. He likes that . . . But at night they're all scared, just like when they were little. Whether they'll be able to bring it to a dignified finish. With such a small pension. And no one has ever come back from there. To tell. Not even her sister. And half of the class is missing, they're no longer with us. And as far as the eye can see, almost no husbands. But in church there's Jesus. But they don't have heating . . . The baby squirmed, sighed, and she sat up, because beware, the cat must take care . . . And she glanced at the clock. We won't do a diaper change, it's almost morning . . . Once, at the very beginning, Paťo said, because later they only talked about how he had slept and whether dinner had sat well with him, that he had gone swimming. And in a huff he added, who's supposed to be looking at that? At what? But he was already in the bathroom. When he walked out, he had the same look as when

44

he had gone in. Why do those old women go to the pool?? Pipina didn't understand. For the same reason you do! And he gaped at her, to look at chicks?

We too have a purpose. We, the ugly. Who don't please ourselves or others . . . She had stopped calling her mother a long time ago. Because there was always a humph . . . Hi mom, I'm just calling because I thought, did, saw, said, so and so. Silence. A teensy-weensy uber-meaningful silence. And then, humph! Wrong. Bad. Pointless. Stupid. Clumsy. All of the above. Full-scale disappoint-ment in Pipina in one short exhalation. They had known one another all her life, they knew each other's every blink, let alone a humph . . . Then came the, Pipi, what if you, wouldn't you like to, couldn't you, perhaps it would be better, I'm sure you know best . . . but that was preceded by the humph. Sarcastic, unfor-tunate, definitive . . . And then she just up and died. And Pipina was alone, day and night, no help in sight, amen! And Pipina humphed like her awful mother . . . His mother sometimes called her. More precisely, she attempted a call, she rang. And after Pipina dropped, set down, closed, turned off everything, because one time she hadn't turned off or closed . . . all this in no more than three or four rings, and ran with her butt naked, or with the baby's butt naked, the mother-in-law would hang up. She wouldn't speak . . . Pipina had no idea why she was doing that. What she was doing. Why she was checking up on her. What was she checking on. Where else should she have been . . . Early on it happened several times a day. It was definitely her. And Pipina swallowed, she had a bad taste in her mouth . . . Pipina was an expert on bad tastes. Bad tastes were her thing! And she started to call her mother-in-law, mother-in-law. A repulsive word. A crumpled word. And the mother-in-law . . . soon had her own keys. The so-called, just-in-case keys. After that she always walked in, and every time Pipina almost had a heart attack. Because she always appeared two feet from them. She didn't yell hello at the door, where are you, don't worry, it's just me, am I disturbing . . . Bad tastes, that was Pipina's thing! Her favourite one was her own.

That was an upside of divorce. The mother-in-law no longer had the keys, just in case, if anything happened . . . That was one good reason Pipina would have wanted the divorce even if he had been really opposed. When you needed her, when you needed a mother-in-law once in a hundred years, because you had no one else in the whole world, and you were leaving because you had to even over dead bodies . . . she would carry the crying baby into the kitchen saying, stop bawling, you've got nooo one to bawl for, you'll figure thaaat out! Or, even your father knows how much troooouble your mother is! Or better still, she doesn't deseeerve you two! Or otherwise, she's not the brightest banaaana in the bunch, you'll seeee! Pipina always recovered only once she was outside . . .

And everyone was on his side. Everyone sided with him. Because she didn't know how to ramble. She always said the first thing that came to her mind. And that was certainly nothing earth shattering. And she was ugly, so she couldn't say whatever she wanted to just so that people could look at her. Up close . . . Sometimes she dreamed about that. That all of a sudden she was, she couldn't put her finger on it, she couldn't describe what had changed about her, she must have been born again, because people were laughing, helping her, stalling, stammering, dropping things, making things up just so she wouldn't leave. Let's breathe together a little longer. The same air. It was in you, and now it's in me! Such folly she dreamed about . . . He was gorgeous day and night. Changing his tone and speech pattern based on who he was talking to. And who was nearby. He always took that into account. In a radius of at least 30 feet. Maybe he wouldn't have been as nice to the person he was talking to if the person who was listening hadn't been there. Maybe he wouldn't have even said what he did had the person who was in earshot not been close by. He had a sixth sense for that. He had a talent for that, for being liked. As much as possible. By as many people as possible. That was his thing. He liked it when they were looking. Can everyone see me? And he knew when they started to pay attention. He could sense who did and who didn't. He perked up, focused on them. And if it didn't work, he gave up. Maybe he'd try once more, maybe twice, he couldn't figure it out, and then he'd get angry. Very consistently, very thoroughly. Very personally. If you don't like me, watch out. I'm keeping an eye on you, you better steer clear of me, go to hell . . . And he didn't like it when one of his people gazed elsewhere. He'd put his full attention on that person. Briefly. He'd overwhelm him . . . The first one he had enslaved was his mother. His father had other things to worry about. It was best to stay out of his way. I'll teach you . . .

To have a good time. An awesome time. To have as good a time as possible at any given moment, that was his goal. So clear, so concise, so simple, so ingenious, it was his lifelong goal. To have as good a time as can be had. At every moment. Right now. At first it was subconscious, then unconscious, then unconsciously premeditated, until it reached consciousness . . . He had only gone grocery shopping once with Pipina, with them, but at least he had an ice cream bar. The woman at the cash register scanned an empty wrapper. That's a new one, she laughed. She would have sent another customer packing, but he was focusing on her . . . That all the kids within 50 feet were begging, but they got a big fat nothing because it was cold and they'd get a sore throat?? I didn't notice! When?? I don't believe you! You think I wouldn't have noticed?? He wasn't bad, just uninhibited. It wasn't personal, just general. To get something out of it. At least a few licks, if he had to carry a bag! Pipina lugged the second one, so he had a free hand. And he didn't even get a sore throat. And the woman at the cash register liked him . . .

Don't touch my mouse with greasy or any other hands. He yelled into the phone once. And speak Slovak. It took her a long time to figure out that the mouse was by a computer and that he was talking to his mother. He didn't waste much time with those who loved him, who couldn't defend themselves. Once in a while he'd caress them, once in a while he'd be in a good mood. They should have been glad. They were . . . And he lied . . . Whenever, about whatever. About big things, as well as trifles. Whatever suited him. When it suited him. Without hesitation. Without thinking. Automatically. For his own protection, defence, comfort, habits, tastes. In short, for his own good. The end justifies the means. The world over, even in history, he said . . . He used the whole world as an excuse, because he needed to like himself. Who knows, maybe it's my mother's fault. He used his mother as an excuse when he ate the first precious cherries. She loved me too much. He hung the last ones over his ears and he was cute as pie. And chomp, chomp, chomp. He only put the last one in her mouth. And she was happy and chomped it down in a flash so that he wouldn't notice her teeth. Awful teeth, nothing-to-speak-of nails, everything's . . . I must have been thirsty. I suppose. Do you know how thirsty I was?? Velvet resounded through the night. It made you gulp. Even his voice was beautiful . . . The second time around he was a little annoyed, he ate the last piece of candy, didn't even leave one for the mother-in-law. And she saw it. And she was upset that he didn't give a damn about them, and that he lied. Me?? Never. When? How dare you! Just ask my mother, though she can't remember anything anyway, carried through the night . . . But it wasn't quite right any more. We're all different, you know. He said to no one in particular. That phoney guilty conscience wasn't working any more. He was getting bored, the halo was fading. He should already have been somewhere else. Don't talk to me like that! He would have felt better at tennis. Healthier. You have to take care of yourself first before you can take care of others. He had an incredible self-preservation instinct. As fabulous as his peripheral vision. And he never let you live it down. He remembered it well. He didn't like it that you knew him . . . New people were the best, new women, guests. He was fantastic at first sight. He loved it, talking about everything. It does a man good for people to know that he has higher goals than some popsicle. That he'd save the Earth, if he could, if they'd listen to him. If they'd only understand. The pricks. He liked strong language, manly, resonant, succinct. Even in front of women. So what? Are they not pricks?? They are pricks. And the women had to shrug their shoulders bashfully . . . And then he was tired and fell asleep. And the women cleaned, it had to be done, it couldn't be helped, with no help . . . When?? I didn't notice that at all. You think I wouldn't have noticed? You didn't tell me, none of you told me . . .

She gave him a key. When she was having it made, she said, it's for my husband, my man. And she was the proudest woman in the world . . . When she was giving it to him, she cast down her eyes, touched that beautiful, tan, muscular hand, and got burned. And she brought it up to her lips and died. And three seconds later she was the happiest woman in the world because she heard them clink in his pocket . . . Not long after, the key was sitting on the cabinet behind the flour. And she said in a thin, cheerful voice, you forgot it in a funny spot. He immediately looked into her eyes, you're the one who dropped it there. And Pipina's porcine eyes stuck out like a snail's, and she turned around. From your pocket, he added . . . And she was the unhappiest woman in the world. Because he lied, and because he didn't want them. The keys to their place, that is . . . And that night he brought it up one last time. You're always home! And you know how tight my jeans are. And you know what? Pipina shook her head in the dark. Maybe my mother didn't bake me a conscience. And she was happy that he actually knew everything, that he felt everything, and he even remembered her joke. Or she had burned it with that great love of hers, burned it in that big baby oven of hers . . . But he didn't wink, that's what you had called it. He had forgotten, it was his now. And she didn't remind him of that nonsense. Really?? When? You don't say . . . That's what he and his friends would call them from now on. They'd be ovens. And some are already baking and others aren't. Either way, they're ovens. And then they're cisterns for some time. You're so funny, Paťo . . .

And at night she blew her nose for the twentieth time, enough already! And she dreamed that she saw a pelican. It must have been. She must have seen it somewhere on TV. It was black and

50

white, with a huge black eye, and big yellow glasses. A strange beak! Made of pink flower petals. The blossoming petals were hugging the pelican's head, narrowing to the beak like a stem. A pink flash, and a fish flailed, reared every which way in the soft sack under the beak. Until the pelican, tossing its head back and forth, got it into the right position, and whoosh, the fish slid into its belly. Through an extremely long neck . . . Pipina only had that dream once. Probably because after the day she had had, she felt like dying. Quickly, easily, usefully! But beware, the cat must take care!!

I'm like his mother. Maybe his mother was ugly too, our protagonist thought, because it takes one to know one. And now all the wrinkles, the skin and bones were covering it up. Maybe she had been beside herself, what a beautiful baby she had, what a clever little boy, what a dashing youth, what a man! That he was holding her finger, that he wanted to ride on her back. Mom, yay! Mom can do it! That when he was as tall as a poplar, he held her around the shoulders. Could there be anything more pleasant? And so that enamoured mother let him think that he was the most important person in the world. Even the moon came to look at you . . . And now our protagonist was trying to tell herself that it was his problem. That everyone's responsible for himself. That he was an adult. That he was a man. That she wouldn't ruin their relationship because of it. That she wouldn't lecture him, scold him, raise him. She was no mother. Not his, anyway . . . Because she wanted to feel good at least for a little while, once in a while. Let him think that life is here just so that Paťko can have a good time. So what? Who knows what life is for anyway, right . . . And she really enjoyed cleaning the toilet. It made her feel like they were a family.

Men just tap theirs. Are you glad? You're glad . . . And she brushed her teeth all the time. In case. Another strong memory. But she didn't remind herself of it, what for . . . How he had kissed her on the lips the first time. How he had grabbed her by the nape of her neck, detestable word, but a lovely move. How his breath melted her, how heat travelled down her body, how her knees went soft, how she was moist all over. Even under her eyelids. That was why she almost never thought about it. She didn't want to be moist under the eyelids . . .

Pipina berated herself. For having unbuttoned the baby's bib. Soon the baby would need it again, and she could have pulled it off over its head. She didn't have the energy to do more than was necessary for them to survive. For them to eat and not be covered in dirt. Because they weren't sleeping. Well, the baby slept. But during the day . . . I really don't understand it! He was right. He really didn't understand it. What his mother tattled to him . . . Because he was handsome, clever, strong, popular, organized. And she was always playing catch up, finishing, barely making it, missed it again, forgot again, cut herself, slipped, it broke, it fell. How can you live like that?? Slapdash . . . Probably because I haven't slept in months. Probably because I have to do everything myself. But she just thought that, with two exclamation points each . . . Careless, half baked, he added in divorce court, completely unnecessarily. The judge was his lovefriend. Lovefriend, yuck!

And it was summer. And the people who think that a man can be uglier than sin and still get to criticize, went out into the streets in the shorts and T-shirts they had been sleeping in all winter. Pipina felt a little nauseous from all that body hair and potbellies on the bus, and she started to understand him. Who could blame a casual man in white, unobtrusive light accents all over, a purse as a colourful touch . . . for thinking he was dressing things up. He smelled good at first sight. Pipina didn't . . . She felt quite embarrassed as she struggled to get off the bus. There wasn't a man or woman who would helf her. Helf was what her awful mother used to say. God knows why, she always thought about her in bad moments. And she managed to break a nail. Pitiful nails, pitiful hair, cellulite. Everything's connected. And the stroller hung . . . over the sidewalk. Because she got caught on the door by a bag handle. She had to do something. So she let go of the stroller . . . it ended pretty well, it landed pretty well . . . she kept an eye on it as she was unhooking herself . . . But she was nervous, so it took a long time. When she finally smiled apologetically at the driver from the sidewalk, he was so enraged that he blurted out and gestured the worst possible things and slammed the door. In a blink her insides tightened into a knot the size of a poppy seed . . . There was another time when Pipina would have deserved it. She had gotten off a bus she had just gotten onto, because she thought she had lost the baby's blanket. It wasn't until she was on the sidewalk that she noticed it hanging off the other side of the stroller. More panic, another 180-degree turn, God knows how, but somehow, besides, she had a ticket . . . But that driver didn't say anything. He was used to it. He wasn't fazed even by such an unimaginable . . . His face only showed basic signs of life. Breathing and blinking . . . It didn't occur to either of them that he should help Pipina. He was a man, and he was at work. For the public.

She and her awful mother had only been by the sea once. And they argued the whole time. Because her mother kept wanting to . . . her mother kept saying . . . swim, breathe, exercise, take advantage of it. The sea *luft*. Her mother used to say *luft* . . . Pipina hated it when her mother went to a parent–teacher conference. There was always fallout. Her mother always blurted out something. Every child's different! But we have to deal with 40 of them! And each one of them different! Aren't you glad? You should be glad! And for a week everyone at school kept saying, aren't you glad, you should be glad . . . By the sea her mother kept telling her what to do the whole time, take off your wet swimsuit, you'll catch cold, pull up your bra, people are coming, read, you're always reading, stop staring, look, too late . . . The thing Pipina remembered most from the whole trip was a couple that had passed them somewhere on the boardwalk. He looked as though he had stepped down from a movie screen, blue eyed with a shirt to match, she was a total sag-butt, dressed like a parrot, with a ragged, dry, orange pony tail . . . And he held a parasol for her as if he were holding an umbrella in a downpour. Concentrating, almost squatting, they made headway against the setting sun and moist breeze. Two butts, one five times larger and more than two feet below the other. And her mother said, heaven knows, there must be something about her . . . And Pipina was afraid her mother would look at her to see whether there wasn't something about her too. But her awful mother just shook her head, we should ask her how she does it . . . And Pipina got scared to death. Her awful mother was capable of asking anyone anything!

She had only seen it once, but she missed it ever since. The sea! No wonder she dreamed about it. Whenever she was in a bad way. Before her high school exit exam, and now. In her dream they were walking down a rocky path. It was a quiet afternoon. Probably Sunday. Everything was bleached by the white sun into colourlessness. The air was still. The glow was still. Only the path wound around. And Pipina stared and stared, when was she going to see it. The sea! A few more steps in the brightness, twice she tripped over silvery rocks she couldn't see in the silvery dust of the hot path, and then it hit her. This was it! The real thing! This was the thing which couldn't fit into her gaze. The thing below must have been water and the thing above was the sky! There was no separation between them! It was impossible to tell where one ended and the other began. The sea and the sky . . . And the whole thing was the colour of your little eyes. Pipina was happy that she had brought the baby into her dream. It was blissfully asleep. They were blissfully gliding down an almost invisible silver path . . . And Pipina squinted, shielded her eyes from the increasingly brilliant brilliance, and all of a sudden she looked back . . . Three feet behind her moseyed a huge car on wide tires. Inaudibly. The chrome teeth were laughing. She veered, moved to the side of the road, stopped. And the esteemed car passed by quietly, slowly, and continued that way for another hundred feet or so, so as not to kick up dust. Only after that did it speed up . . . A big black limousine behind it did the same thing, and then two more. And not one of them honked. So as not to wake the baby. Its little sea eyes . . .

Pipina knew why she had dreamed about that! Because yesterday on their afternoon walk they had wandered off further than usual. And Pipina didn't know the treacherous terrain there, and unwisely, she wanted to cross the road. But on the other side there was an incomprehensible curb. She had never seen such a high curb in her life. And she couldn't climb up onto the sidewalk. The underside of the stroller got stuck. The poor thing creaked like an old ship and wouldn't budge. She kept tugging on it in a nervous frenzy, cars kept whizzing by, and the drivers kept shaking their heads at that . . . The frightened baby cried all the way home, and she saw two heads in bed . . . They entered the apartment, walked into the room, and found two heads sleeping in bed . . . Facing each other. Nose to nose . . . As if they had been carved, chiselled by a wood carver, they reflected off the white pillow . . . Petrified, she backtracked, shh, quiet, shh, they're sleeping, shh, shh . . . And out of that cheek, out of that tiny mouth that had covered the image which had already impr-assed itself in her mind, also came out a shh and a tiny bubble . . .

Pipina didn't stop until she was at the playground. And she realized that she actually felt relieved . . . It was too much of an adrenaline sport for a beginner like her. To sleep at attention, without a pillow, so as not to get makeup on everything. Cell phone by her head to wake up first and brush her teeth . . . She didn't believe there were many loves in the world that could survive a morning kiss without a toothbrush. Not that she was hoping, but she wouldn't have been able to think about anything other than her bad breath. She also showered after he was already asleep and when he was still asleep. Not that she was hoping, but she wouldn't have survived, she would have killed herself, had she stunk. If she had realized it after the fact . . . In short, it was way too much anxiety for four lovemakings in history, in their whole history . . . But the biggest trauma was the toilet. In the middle of a panel-construction apartment, without any soundproofing, yet impossible to air out. She didn't have the strength to go in there when he was home. She must have never grown up, she was embarrassed to make sounds. For the first few days. After that he didn't linger . . . Even peeing resounded throughout the apartment. But that could be solved at the sink, with running water. Sometimes she wondered why he ever showed up. He must have been tired, and his mother would have asked questions. Like a surgeon or a politician, who needs to get a good night's rest once in a while. Without probing questions . . . They'd have a very short conversation in the morning, how did he sleep, did he enjoy dinner, and then muah, muah, both in the air, he ran out . . . Only once did he ask, how are you two? We're, we have our fir-fir-first smile! Pipina stammered in surprise. The baby looked at me yesterday, and, and, and . . . Of course the baby was looking like they were talking about someone else. What do you know . . . Right. Right . . . And muah, muah, both in the air, he ran out . . . And she was happy for half the day, and several times she even chanted out loud, may you inherit his, may you inherit his! Your daddy has the most beautiful smile in the world! So vulnerable! And she finally went to the toilet. Then and there she ripped her bra out of all the creases it had cut into. She left the door open. Naturally, she was in the habit of leaving the door open to hear every breath, whimper, smack. So that was what she had just lost . . . He never put down the toilet seat. Perhaps as a reminder that he had been there. Like a dog that marks its territory. Or perhaps so she'd remember his . . . She liked that. So that was what she had just lost . . .

So she saw, they saw two heads. The following night she didn't sleep at all. And the only thing that helped her was thinking about why she'd have to leave him, even if he really didn't want her to . . . He had shouted a couple of times. At the baby. It had been annoying him. He didn't try to figure out why, he just shouted.

For it to act normal! Like a normal human being! The baby . . . When it happened for the third time, and the baby was staring at him with its eyes like plums because daddy was telling it to behave . . . the baby . . . for the first and perhaps the last time in her life she wished he were dead. Oh, there was another time, one night he rose up from the covers like a giant, blind worm and shouted SILENCE, because the baby had a tummy ache . . . But she immediately said to herself that there's justice in the world, and she'd certainly die first . . . Though, come to think of it, it would be great from an educational perspective. She could always say how obedient daddy was and what a great student he was! No, seriously, she could always talk about what daddy dear would have done, helped with, taken care of. He could never say no to anyone and he always felt up to everything. But above all, he loved us very much. And he always held everything for everyone, carried things even though it was out of his way and he didn't have the time, but above all, he loved us very much. And we talked about everything, though most of all about you. The way you smiled for the first time. And he said, impossible! And I said, it is possible, and he said, I don't believe you, and I said, I swear, and he said, hats off. But above all, he loved us very much . . . And one time he walked out of the house in his bathrobe, because he had been comforting you all morning because you had been a little sick, and also because he never looked in the mirror, and we saw it from the window, but we let him be. And we grinned. But he didn't get mad, he smiled most beautifully in the whole world. Completely vulnerably. And he loved us very much. And he had incredible peripheral vision and an impressive ability to hold it, which he mentioned every now and then, but above all, he loved us very much . . . He had only gotten angry once in his life. On a walk, one of many, we always took walks together. With you in the middle. We were holding hands and we were proud of how well you had turned out . . . So, he had only gotten angry once, when someone was beating a child on its head. You must have been beaten on the head too, to be so stupid. He said in such a manner that all of us almost po . . . ourselves from fear. Including that stupid lady who had first let her kid run amok. In all seriousness, it would be an incredible educational tool. Pipina could say wonderful things she had seen elsewhere, read from the smartest people, and the baby would stuff them into its little head forever, because its wonderful daddy had said them. The one who was in heaven. Do you see that little star? He'll always be there, and he'll always be looking out for you. Nothing bad can happen to you, because he loves you very much. Forever . . . What an upbringing that would be! With one hand tied behind your back, as Paťo would say.

So he filed for divorce. Maybe because she had asked him for help. Because before the baby can walk, something should be done about that . . . She hadn't said a word about the chiselled heads on the white pillow. And the baby only said grr . . . She didn't cry until she was struggling to secure those shelves by herself. It felt as though they could still be pulled down. That was why she was crying . . . Either way, Tuesday is better than Monday. A lot better, and tomorrow's already Wednesday. And then it's almost Friday. But why was she looking forward to Saturday? It must have been some habit from childhood. Probably because there was no school. Because every day is the same. Because life is just a series of good and bad moments. And some that are neither here nor there. But those are bad too . . . And good-looking people have good moments . . . surely . . . and ugly people have ugly moments and some that are neither here nor there. And in one of them you die . . . Like her awful mommy. And that's that.

Sometimes you get mad at a baby. When you're tired, exhausted. But when you steal a kiss, when you press up against that tiny back, you feel like the baby's helping you. With its warmth, with its scent. Like it's sheltering you in its safe, all-important little world. Where you belong one million per cent. In the middle of the dangerous, gigantic world where you can't find your place at all . . . When the baby holds onto you with its strong little hand, where it reaches, you're precious, you are! And Pipina dozed off . . . And she had a teeny-tiny dream about the sea. They were on a beach. And the waves were crashing on rocks, splashing, rushing, roaring. And the baby was making fun of them from its stroller, as if from a kitchen window. It imitated them as loudly as it could. In her dream it was already sitting up! And Pipina collected pebbles, shells, and walked around barefoot on the sand. I wish I had that dream all the time . . . And when she came back, the baby laughed. So they played that way. The baby wasn't scared when she was leaving, it was just happy to see her come back.

Two envy-worthy people. Pipina envied them like crazy. Something should be done about that! I should do something about that, envy consumes beauty . . . He had great legs in the shape of an O, and a great grin permanently carved into his face by great wrinkles. The best white ones around his eyes were only occasionally visible . . . She had breast-like protrusions all over. B's under her shoulder blades, C's above her waist, B's under her waist, C's under her butt, B's on her arms, C's in one armpit . . . B's moving to C's in the other armpit. Golden sandals on her bunioned feet. Both of them over eighty. They were having a blast on an ordinary walk . . . They didn't need anyone, but they were interested in everyone. And they pointed everything out to one another, exchanged, lent, smelled, marvelled. And Pipina envied them like crazy . . . And he picked her up and carried her over a puddle. A regular strong man under 90. She didn't thank him at all, it was matter of course. But she held his . . . cell phone. I'd enjoy being old too. Guilt free and footloose in a beautiful place with a beloved person. For a few years. And then dream the eternal dream side by side. No, seriously . . . Pipina was convinced that they slept together. And she didn't mind imagining it a little.

She got caught up in a conversation by the dumpsters. With an older, but better-looking woman than herself. They each took out the trash with similar frequency, so Pipina thought she also lived alone. She was hobbling. Pipina said hello, a little help would be nice, wouldn't it . . . Men?? Trash?? Take out?? Resounded clearly, unequivocally, harshly. Don't be naive! It sounded as uncompromising as a statement from a podium. The most important thing is not to ask them for anything! Especially not anything concrete. They get scared shitless. The dumpster echoed. They feel threatened. Their guard goes up immediately, her words carried through the neighbourhood. They don't even know why yet, but they're already afraid! That you may need something. Something specific, specifically from them! The woman was obviously just getting started. Most importantly, not anytime soon! Tomorrow?? You can't be serious! Today?? That would send them over the edge! They're lazy as lice. A mosquito net?? He got very sad. And that was right after we had fallen in love. You have to take care of, figure out, and arrange everything yourself while maintaining the appearance that you're lost without him, and then he'll forgive you anything, even a flat chest . . . If his comfort becomes as sacred to you as it is to him, plus good cooking, he won't ever leave you, not even for a 15-year-old. That's what you should keep in mind instead of rifling through their pockets and their cell phones. You may not cook like mommy, but you also don't nag him the way she does. I said that to him once, but now he thinks it's his own opinion. The fact that a mosquito net had been acquired and put up, that slipped right past him. It's just comfy here. Have you noticed that there are no mosquitoes in our house? And of course, once in a while you've got to give him some. And pretend it's the one thing you've been waiting for. That it's the only thing you expect out of life. Then the neighbour hobbled away. She fell. She tied something somewhere . . . And you have to tell the kids, daddy's home. Nothing bad can happen to us now, he's hooome . . . But shhh, don't bother him, he's watching the news . . . the wind carried her words . . . And Pipina laughed all the way to her kitchen. She knew that in those ten minutes she had gotten a PhD in marriage, but she didn't heed the advice and asked him to take out the trash. It reeked, and it was late, and she couldn't get the baby to sleep . . . It wasn't clear whether he had heard her, but all of a sudden he had a strange feeling. It reeked in there, and Pipina had her hands full. And he thought about his mother, who used to take out the trash in the morning when she went to pick up the groceries, automatically. I need to go by my mother's. He got up, I have a strange feeling she may need something. You know, she's all alone, and he was gone . . . She didn't even have a chance to tell him, if you're headed out, could you please . . .

And Pipina dreamed about a road! Made of small cobblestones. A fine old lady of a road. One fan pattern after another, it descended towards an old house. A fine old gentleman of a house. And the road fanned him all the way to the empty swimming pool.

A fine old gentleman of a swimming pool. Next to it stood fine, old, but slender lady vases. Everything was made of white marble, full of wrinkles. Even the couple of short, rounded steps leading to the terrace were wrinkly. The terrace as well . . . With a few metal lace tables and chairs. That looked like Dalmatians. Sitting up straight without any effort. Their black spots were rust . . . And the façade of the house gleamed behind them. Palm-sized pieces of glass were assembled into French doors. And Pipina couldn't resist, she pressed her face up against them. A room the size of the whole house. A few columns of golden dust in the golden rays of the setting sun. A golden dusk, and sofas, couches, pillows, all the same colour. And two enormous bouquets of yellow roses . . . Pipina walked past three sets of windows, tapping their lead veins with her fingertips, and then she snuggled up to them again. Through the thick panes she could see a piano, a harp, and a giant golden cage. No one was in the cage either. And Pipina said to herself, why are you surprised, how else should things look in a dream? Like this!

Yesterday she struggled to get the stroller off the bus again, and no one helped her. There was only a laughing gaggle of teenagers and the driver. The teenagers were in their own world, the driver in his. He stared intently into his briefcase. When things were taking a while, he stuck his hand in it. Then he shot a glance outside. Because she had farted from all that effort. You see, Paťo, my peripheral vision is almost as good as yours . . . And then a person came to her aid. She was so thin and so pale that Pipina hadn't noticed her before. And the poor thing twisted her ankle on the second step, and they all tumbled until they landed on the sidewalk . . . Pipina was straightening things, fixing the stroller, the baby, and that poor woman sat down right there, on the ground . . . The freed bus angrily slammed its doors, blew stench into their faces, heaved, and took off. And Pipina had no idea what to do. She kept repeating, I hope, it's not too, I just hope, you're not too . . . And the itty-bitty person asked, may I? And she tied Pipina's shoelace. Since she was already there, right around, on the ground . . . And Pipina didn't know what to do, she just kept repeating, I'm sorry, I'm so sorry. Don't worry, it happens to me all the time . . . Then the itty-bitty person pulled herself up by the stroller and said, the baby's sleeping so beautifully, and she hobbled away . . .

They were at the park. The nearest one. Pipina didn't like going there, it was a sad place. It was pitiful. Neglected. Only used. Abused . . . All Pipina needed was to hear where she could find a second-hand store for baby clothes. But she wasn't interested in making friends. It always ended with, let's have coffee, one day at my place, one day at yours. Not at my place, my . . . So she just said hello at the entrance, but no one noticed her. She should have turned around then and there, the conversation was certainly not going to be about second-hand stores . . . On the bench closest to her sat two women, talking, piled over with everything one can be piled over with at a playground. And all of it was pink. Except for two white cigarettes balanced on a teensy-weensy pink ashtray. It was too small for them . . . Pipina looked around, trying to find the little girls. It took her a while. Because they were quiet and just stood there. Then one of them bent down with an outstretched arm, but she changed her mind, and they stood some more . . . My husband and I had such a good laugh a couple of days ago, what did you eat at daycare? A woll. What roll?? Like this. And the wife showed an inch with her fingers. She's so cute, laughed the other one, my goodness, you'll fatten her up now. No way, we'll only cook in the evenings, it's summer vacation. Lunch will be sandwiches or Mickey D's. Oh, the other one nodded, no longer laughing. Look, mom . . . Yesterday my husband and I had a party, I turned 34. Mom, look. We had such a good time, my husband's colleagues wished me a happy 24th. Mom, look. I'm not surprised at all . . . said the one who was no longer laughing. Soon people will think you and your daughter are sisters. Mom. Look. And Pipina said, show me . . . They turned towards her like two birds of a feather. Angry ones, too. And it got quiet . . . And in that quiet, the little pink pale doll stuck her hand behind her back, Pipina waved goodbye, and she left as fast as her feet would carry her. She heard the wife telling the doll, you promised not to get dirty! I'll never trust you again . . . Life's shit! It was Pipina who said that.

And she dreamed about a pink street. Pipina knew exactly why it was that colour. The two-or-so-storey houses were made of brick. The sun had bleached them pink. Acacia trees lined the street. They were as tall as the houses. But the acacia leaves and sprigs were so fine, they were practically invisible. At the same time, thousands of clusters of pink flowers hung in plain sight . . . People as well as Pipina with the stroller waded through the acacia scent. And Pipina squatted down to bring her head to the baby's level, where the scent was too heavy. So she brought the baby up to where the scent was lighter. Just right . . . A woman walked by, and her husband said, you only carry us in your arms for a short while. Why is that? Because you're only good for a short while, the woman replied. They thought the baby was a boy.

She envied and she couldn't help it. She envied couples. Anywhere, anytime. And she watched them. In the supermarket, on the bus. The other day she made a funny mistake. Two people were standing in line at the cash register, and the man's trouser pocket was badly torn. Why won't she mend that for him?? Of course, they went their separate ways, but Pipina had already thought the worst of the woman. What a pity, they looked good together, and he needed to be taken care of . . . There was one time she didn't envy. They were both dressed in black. Not in mourning, Parisian style! Tall and elegant, they walked out of a store like two gazelles . . . Reflecting with their beautiful packages off the beautiful doors . . . Which Pipina didn't dare approach. She no longer risked such things. Disparaging glares of lone shop girls, who were right, as always. She couldn't have bought anything anyway. Do they not sell handkerchiefs, Pipi? Her awful, naive mommy would have asked . . . And Mr Perfect, whose scent wafted over on a breeze, said to Mrs Perfect, whose scent wafted over as well . . . Pipina could picture those intertwining scent ornaments as if they had been drawn in a comic strip . . . if you correct me one more time in front of someone, I'll shove a broomstick up your cunt and keep twisting it, you bitch. She only said one word to him. It rhymed with stick. And her face gleamed white.

The next day a series of accidents happened in the kitchen. Everything was falling, clattering, spilling. Because she was doing everything at once. Because everything should have been done already, because they had overslept. She ended up sitting on the floor with the rescued baby whimpering in her arms, because she wouldn't give it the thing that had started the whole mess. A darn ladle! But with sharp edges! She couldn't let the baby have it right off the floor! She did . . . And then she trembled like jello. Her awful mother would have said like aspic. And on their walk they ran into that girl, the head! Chiselled to perfection and now made up as well! Pipina knew there was trouble, so she kept staring into the stroller. The girl walked with them for at least 20 minutes. She kept looking around. Pipina wondered whether she was hoping they were on their way to meet Pato. For a second she felt proud, but that was stupid. Each of them was just . . . another day, another play . . . The girl kept laughing so loud it would make you flinch. Pipina's index finger flew up to her lips twice, shh-shh, because the baby was sleeping. And everything was cool, or intense, or gross. And people looked good or like shit. Pipina felt so embarrassed. And they were either hot, or if over 40, fucked up. The whole street had to hear about it. And it consumed three cigarettes, and the girl tossed the butts in an arc to show her contempt for the world. Sickening! Finally, in lieu of a goodbye, she said all men are pricks, lit up another one, and left . . . Pato had said that once. Who knows which one of them had said it first . . . And evening was unbearably far away . . .

Sometimes the baby would grab onto her tight, like a little monkey. And she'd cuddle it. She'd never dare hug it by force. The teeny-tiny person. Not a big one either . . . And tears welled up in her eyes. Because she didn't have . . . a more beautiful shadow, a better taste, a better . . . He doesn't give a damn about you, get that through your thick skull already! He's with someone else now, even if you died! He wouldn't notice! You don't looook and you don't aaact like a woman, her mother-in-law said once. And do you know what has ruuuined you. She didn't even bother with a question mark. Your cooomplexes. Millions of your cooomplexes.

The mother-in-law was dredging in hard truths. And your pride. Though I can't imagine what you've got to be proud ooof!! Why should you, of all people, be his ooonly one? My husband used to come home half drunk. God knows where he'd been. I told him he drank ooonly once. He got offended and came home drunk agaaain. So I stopped noticing. From the couch he directed which home appliance to turn down, turn off, or tune. And hand me that. And take this, since you're already uuup . . . He used to play with Paťo back then too. Sitting. As looong as it could be done sitting. Actually, he was in the best mood when he had haaad a few. They say a person's reeeal character comes through after he's had a few, so why make a fuuuss . . . That reminded Pipina that she didn't want to be nagging him either, so they'd have as many nice moments as possible . . . At least while sitting.

Finally it was evening again. And she was resting on the friendly staircase in her favourite twilight. Then she entered her striped apartment. She liked that too. The apartment full of familiar stripes. Which were pulled along and returned into place by each passing car. The domestic animal was breathing. Evening was the best part of the day . . . And like almost every night, almost night after night, before she turned on the lights, she enjoyed the moment . . . In the building across from her lived a tall, dark, somewhat clumsy, somewhat slow young man. One whose mind it never crossed to be embarrassed. One who only closed his blinds when he could sleep in. Just so he could sleep in the next day. One who undressed in the middle of the room and had a big one. Like everything else. He was a big, slow, grown boy. And he was thinking about something and caressing it. He caressed it like a kitten. After all, he was at home. And it was night time. And Pipina also felt she had reached a well-deserved end of her day . . . Sex had only crossed her mind the first time. When she thought that he didn't have blinds. That it was a sin to look. After that she just watched him tenderly as he set out his shirt, underwear, and socks for the next day. Incredibly slowly for her hectic, overworked taste. With his large, careful hands he caressed, smoothed, folded, and straightened everything. That big grown boy liked to touch everything . . . On Sundays he sometimes stood in the sunshine by the open window and read. And caressed it. Mindlessly. And Pipina felt peaceful too. That boy made her feel calm. Briefly she wasn't afraid.

She dreamed that she was going on a date. She didn't know with whom, but she knew when and where. And how to get there. And one other thing was certain; she had nothing to wear. Teary-eyed . . . I'll have puffy eyes to boot . . . in an old mirror she saw an armoire behind her. Worn to perfection, like parquet floors in a dance hall. It went on and on. And it curved. There were drawers everywhere, polished by use. Big ones, as well as minuscule ones. Half-closed, ajar, the closest one was full of gloves, full of imagination. Some were like spider webs, others like woodcarvings. They'd be too small anyway. All of them! And Pipina cried. Because she didn't have a grandmother. Because she didn't have an old armoire smoothed by white hands she had known forever. And their hand cream. After every Sunday dinner, after doing the dishes, they had to be taken care of, the nails had to be filed like tiny almonds . . . In the morning her pillow was wet, and her mood to start the day was worse than usual. Stupid dreams! Good thing grandma didn't live to see where I've ended up. She died before Pipina didn't grow out of it. We're cut from the same cloth, she used to say. Women should be like daisies. All different! But always brave. She used to say. But there are no ugly flowers!

This was another dumpster acquaintance. After all, where else did Pipina go?? The baby was sleeping at home, the window was open, and Pipina stopped every ten steps, held her breath, and listened. Not a peep! Then they stood there for at least an hour, because Pipina hadn't seen a living soul for two days, let alone another adult. But every ten minutes they held their breaths and listened. There's an excuse for everything, just not for a child, right?? What a nice person! She started to talk right away, holding nothing back . . . She said she was incredibly lucky, because she had a wonderful husband, a bear. And Pipina was ensnared, she loved couples and their stories. She envied so beautifully. She had herself a nice envy session, but every ten minutes they took a breath . . . He loves me, because I'm so tiny. And I wear high heels a size too small. I torture myself, but I'm adorable. And I don't let him drive me to work! Do you know the adventures you can have on trams and buses?? When I'm on a roll, I don't even stamp my ticket. Adventure lies around every corner. Right now my biggest one happens here, by this dumpster. Pipi wasn't catching on with her mouth open. Recently I met a guy here, upside down. Pipi covered her mouth with her little paw. I was fishing my trashcan out of the dumpster. It's the sort of thing that can only happen to me, I do everything lickety-split, willy-nilly, helter-skelter, I was lucky I didn't end up in there myself. He saved me. At the last minute he grabbed my butt. And that was it. I couldn't get over that grab, that manoeuvre, the way he caught me. Pipina choked on her own spit . . . The woman hit her on the back. He kept me there a moment longer, upside down, but I knew I was safe, we both knew that was just for fun. Pipina waved her arms to signal that she was OK, she didn't want to miss a thing. He said I have a great rear end, and that he's an expert on such matters. And when he tipped me over, that is, when he set me on the ground, I mean, right side up, he said, you're pink like, I'd like to say panties, but I'll say cotton candy. I blushed all the way home. Pipina blushed too, like she was being paid for it. Then they took a breath and listened . . . not a peep! The next time he was there waiting for me. In the elevator I had repeated out loud the exact time I had met him, so that I'd remember, and there he was again, so what was I to do. He pushed me here behind this bush with one hand. I love it when men don't ask questions. What for, right? And when they know how to do it. Pipina knew there was a bench behind the bush, but she had no idea it had such an eventful history. The panties came off, and that was that. Done, Pipina whispered. Panties back up, and hooray home. The woman shook her head, tucked her hair behind her ears, and smiled innocently. But don't think for an instant I'm hurting my husband, he loves me just the way I am! Afterwards I'm in a good mood, I come up with all sorts of things, I put on bows, I cook, I sing to him, and he's happy. He's quite good looking! He was a basketball player when he was young! You know how that goes, back then young women threw themselves at him, they followed him around, all he had to say was, in front of the stadium and the time. When he stopped playing, he became a coach, so it was enough to say, after practice. Poor thing, he didn't have time for more. So then he was out of practice, and he didn't know how to talk to women. It wasn't enough any more just to slap them on a thigh and mumble something unintelligible. But I wasn't shy, and I bagged him, I bagged him for myself, the poor thing. That's what I call him! You poor thing. He calls me his turtledove. Some turtledove you are! Maybe he knows! I named the time and the place. The woman raised her arms above her head and stood on tiptoe. I've got a damn good husband. As big and strong as a bear. And I snuggle up to him, you poor thing, you, and he says, no, no, no, and I say, yes, yes,

yes, you know, foreplay . . . Because I have a good personality, you see. Easy going. I used to think that beauty was the most important thing. Bullshit! The most important thing is personality. The easier the better. Don't you think so, no, no? And Pipi nodded her head yes, yes, but then she remembered that it was foreplay, so she stopped. Wow. She was impressed, and she envied her all the way home. That woman really wasn't particularly good looking. But she had that easy-peasy personality . . . As incomprehensible as pink panties or cotton candy.

This was another neighbour. She was talking on the phone on her balcony. Where else would Pipina go! The baby was asleep. I was going out with this asshole. Pipina couldn't see her, she could only hear. You have to have sex with someone before you start talking. Pipina didn't know whether she had heard wrong, but she immediately envied the definitive stance. It was a mistake, he scared away all the others. Including the interesting one. We played truth or dare . . . Have you ever had sex without love?? It was a personal question. I was a little bit in love, since we were sleeping together, but more importantly, he was there! No, never! They got me. I was no longer interesting. Because it sounded like we were already talking. With that asshole! And they knew he was an asshole because they played tennis with him. He doesn't play, he talks about it, the interesting one said. We had started to talk a little, hence the personal question . . . So I'm married to an asshole. With no sex. They were right. He talks about it . . . Pipina quietly left the balcony and headed for the kitchen. Where else would Pipina go! And as she walked through the door, a cockroach crawled out of the drain. They looked at one another. It had been there once before . . . That time Pipina pretended not to see it. This time it was impossible. All Pipina could muster was shoo, shoo, and she lost it. From then on she was always going to be scared to walk into the kitchen. She was no longer in charge there . . . And outside, on a beaten-up lilac tree hung a huge garden spider. How come those who had done it weren't scared of it? The spider must have been smarter than all of them put together, it hung itself there after everything had already been lopped off. It must have had a hiding spot somewhere, like the cockroach. That wasn't someplace Pipina would want to be! They were simply smarter, stronger, because they were millions of years older. Therefore she feared them, the way every primitive fears his betters.

It was really windy on that overpass. The wind blew right at you, right into your face. The baby was cold too. Pipina hurried, using the stroller as a wind bulldozer. She looked back and saw a fragile grandpa wobbling behind her on crutches. He looked at her, you're as evil as you're ugly, and he averted his eyes. As usual, Pipina's stomach tightened into a knot the size of poppy seed. I'm a scarecrow inside and out. A bogeyman . . . There was a gust of wind, and she remembered something cheerful. A child at the playground kept eating sand. The others just tried it, but this one couldn't get enough of it. Undeterred, it crawled towards the sandbox over and over again. And it got very angry every time its mother dusted off its hands. And the next day the mother said, we made a poo-poo instead of a castle. Picture not making a sand castle but a sand poo. All the mothers laughed . . . And Pipina turned around, the poor man was struggling right behind her. First she slowed down, then she let him win. He turned towards Pipina victoriously, but he didn't raise a crutch in celebration. In the cold, only the baby's eyes were sticking out of the stroller. They didn't even blink so as not to miss anything.

When she was very tired, she couldn't remember words. For some reason, the most difficult ones were acorn, notary, and craft. And most recently, chameleon. She had no idea why. She didn't even know why she needed those words in particular. Now she couldn't even remember her own name, she had had a rough night . . . The baby was a little sick. It didn't eat or sleep, it was snotty. Too much snot for too small of a nose. And Pipina told herself out loud, it's pointless, we should just stick it out, but she didn't stick it out, and they went to see the doctor. But they didn't make it . . . They were walking on a sidewalk, they were just walking on a sidewalk as usual, and a herd of staggering voc-tech students came towards them. They were saying ugly things loud enough for the whole street to hear. And Pipina thought, she had taught it to them. Missing teeth, worn out clothes, stains all over . . . She tightened her grip on the stroller handle and went on. And the boys walked around her . . . but each of them reached. They found her invisible breasts, her front, and her rear. Of course you're glad! This one seemed especially glad, such a beauty! Give it to her good, don't slack off, she needs it too! She wants you . . . She didn't know who said what, but it stank to high heaven. Their breaths. And they passed . . . and neither they nor she had stopped . . . Lucky for them they didn't touch the stroller. She would have killed them.

It was Pipina's birthday. And no one knew about it. And no one said happy birthday to her. She was alone. But a million times more vulnerable because of the baby. Like the proud little tree that had been looking around the other day and rustling with at least 20 new leaves, the show-off! But it was thin . . . And so the following day found it broken at the waist. What could be more defenceless than a little tree at night? And Pipina lifted its top, put it where it used to be, and she cried. There was nothing to be done . . . Pipina didn't know what to do to make that festive day be finally over . . . And she dreamed about a gate. A huge, shiny, dark, wooden gate. The gate boomed, slid open, and light poured out. Beyond a hall the size of a meadow, the sun was setting into a bay. And in that sea halo, an angel-like silhouette materialized. In a miniskirt. High heels in hand . . . And the angel wiggled its nose, and a person in white was unloading a van that was lying next to the sidewalk like a white shadow, pulling out white vases with tall white orchids. They smelled good! And then we were all counting the delicate stems out loud. One for each year. When it gets dark, there's going to be a huge birthday party . . . All done, and the gate started to close, only the star of the keyhole was shining, and the white car was no longer lying next to the sidewalk . . . She's my age and she has everything, but she doesn't have a baby. It was smiling at her from under her arm . . .

She had no patience for it. She hated it. Children's crazy love! Little people love without limits, unconditionally, the way they breathe, the way they need them . . . their big people. Big people can do whatever they want with their little ones, because the little ones have nothing but them. Nothing but their big people . . . She walked into a supermarket with the baby. The door closed behind them and then it opened again, and a child's crying ran in. Pipina turned around. He was less than three-feet tall, mom was close to six. And she was pretty. In an athletic way. From up high, she looked around nimbly like a giraffe. But she wasn't nice. Nothing could faze her. Least of all the little boy, snot and tears down to his waist, literally, screaming in every direction, daddy, daddy. He's in the back, she said slowly. Strangely enough, the little boy understood where in the back was and he ran that way. Mom stayed a few feet behind him with her long, leisurely steps. And the little boy cried, screamed, darted. The store was like a stadium for him. Everyone kept turning around, and that brave boy kept being mistaken. That's not daddy, not that, and that's not daddy either! Pipina stood there, not believing her own eyes at how overjoyed and then how disappointed the boy was each time. Damn it, where's that dad!! And in that hushed store, the mother slowly turned around to look at her, everything stopped, and the boy found his father . . . In the farthest corner of the supermarket, the right face turned towards him. The boy flew up on him, climbed up to his throat all by himself. It was a matter of life and death. And that tall man caressed his little back, what's wrong, what's wrong, what's going on, what happened, did something happen to you? And the store resumed its noise level, its motion, and the boy sobbed around that giant's neck . . . Pipina didn't get it. Maybe the father's deaf! But what kind of a mother is that? What is she trying to raise, a sniper?? Or is she settling some unfathomable divorce/insulted/toxic score with the father?? Pipina couldn't get over it. She hated it! That all-forgiving children's love. The important thing was that they were together again. Holding hands tightly. The little hand had turned white! And the boy turned around, he was looking for his mother . . .

This was one hell of a store! It was the day after tomorrow, and they were standing in line at the checkout again. An irate queue of carts and people. Suddenly a man bent down, quick as lightning. He swooped down like an eagle onto a little boy . . . In frozen time, in complete silence, a small voice died down . . . I'd like. Probably not the first time. The little boy must have needed it the way only little boys can need something. With all their might and right now . . . And the big nose and the little nose were half an inch apart, and the wide-eyed little boy instantly covered his cheeks. Then he moved his hands to his ears and back again. He wasn't able to cover it all at once with those little hands. Finally he settled on the ears, because there was a hiss, you want me to smack your ears . . . Time stood still for another second until the man stood up again, as if nothing had happened. And nothing had, we were all looking . . . And the little boy kept looking at his shoes, his small arms hung motionlessly . . . And you can sympathize with that dad, it's got to be a trip, such power! It's got to be, to be at least a hundred times stronger and bigger! And to hit or not to hit, depending on the mood! Depending on how his day had been at work! Where he's completely small.

They went to the pitiful, but nearest park. And Pipina got excited. She saw it from afar. That most wonderful, most private sight. There was a mother nursing! On one of the two surviving benches. Not that you could see a breast, they were just curled up in that loving ball . . . And the path went by them, and of course Pipina wasn't looking, but even so she spotted another little head behind mommy's back. Only the top of the head was sticking out, it was snuggling, as close as possible, up to mommy's back. Stop hanging on me! Do you know how heavy you are?? Go somewhere! The top of the head froze, then a serious face popped up. He could have been of school age. You're a big kid now! And the little boy left, embarrassed. Until, thank goodness, he saw a wheel sticking out of the sand . . . He wasn't big, he just knew a lot already. For example, that he was alone. During nursing? The little boy lifted his wise head. Maybe he could snuggle up after?

An unmerciful night. A battle over every gulp! The baby didn't want her at all, yet it kept crying from hunger. She didn't know what was going on, until she finally grasped the real problem. The highest rejection on the rejection thermometer. A man, that's just 99.5°F! At most 100°F! She ended up expressing her milk and giving it to the baby from a bottle. It drank. A little. But Pipina knew it was a road to hell. That it would end with formula! And when she stuck a thermometer up the baby's little rear end, it pooped all over everything. Liquid. The baby was sick . . . And in the morning she gave a tired grin. For some reason, not just the baby, but she too had everything on the wrong way. Shirt inside out and backwards. And the baby chirped loudly about it and just wanted to play. Everything was perfectly fine, the eating and the poop . . . Pipina was happy, but she felt like a rag with no energy to battle a new day. And she had to put everything back in order, wipe, wash, deal with, by the sweat of her brow, alone. At least do a first pass. And she didn't even have anyone she could tell about it. She was done for like a cockroach, like their cockroach. Maybe it also fell asleep that afternoon . . . Once again she was pushing the stroller uphill. The road was full of potholes. Full of scars. And she heard the bus, but she was out of breath. She was embarrassed because people were staring at her, and the lit-up bus was standing on the hill with its doors flung open. Then a man ran ahead of her, and a woman behind him yelled, Jozef, take care of it! The bus coughed, growled, the doors slammed shut, and everyone on the street froze. Only Jozef turned towards his Mrs like reproach personified, hat in hand. And the bus growled some more and angrier, and the audience's eyes were popping out of their heads. Because it wasn't sinking over the hill, because it was getting bigger and bigger, until it huffed right at Pipina's feet. And a good-looking driver sprung out of his seat, jumped over the pole separating him from the rest of us, would you like some help? He and Jozef loaded the stroller onto the bus like it was a feather . . . And then some little miss offered her a seat. Unfortunately, it was impossible to refuse. Even though Pipina didn't like to sit . . . looking at the private parts of the people who were standing. Other than that, it was a nice dream, and she wanted to remember it. But when she cracked her eyes open, her gaze landed on the crib . . . the baby wasn't there! She pried them open, hurled herself onto all fours . . . the baby was stuck in the opposite corner! It wasn't pressed into its usual corner, but into the opposite one! And it was breathing! Snoozing comfortably, stuffed into a completely different corner than usual . . . But by then a million neurons as well as the dream had gone to he—in a ha—as her awful mother used to say. She hadn't even taught her to swear properly! Nothing to give her some relief. Awful mother!

Pipina dreamed. The worse, the better. The worse things got, the better her dreams. Colourful. Widescreen. And she was in! In a fog. In turquoise. And dew twanged off a tree, making spider webs vibrate far and wide. All of them jingled with droplets. Pipina didn't know they were everywhere. From every blade of grass to every flower, from every twig to every raspberry, hung a Christmas string. Billions of droplets vibrated, shimmered. A little bird whizzed by, and some of the teardrops couldn't hold on any longer, they dripped down. They fell, rolled through a tiny crack into the ground. Directly to some thirsty root. She could almost hear that unimaginably soft sucking . . . And one of the spider webs let go on one side, and pearl by pearl, in slow motion, the whole string set down into the moss. Every one of them winked . . . And in the midst of that emerald blue wet greenery stood a large white house.

Solid, faithful, built for a family. On the ground floor, a breeze was combing through a field of daisies, which were turned towards the sun like sunflowers. With elegant twirls they bowed in the wind like folk dancers . . . And above them and the breeze was another white floor with large windows, so clean they looked as though they didn't have glass. White pillowy clouds floated across them . . . The house must have had a flat roof, because Pipina was sunbathing on it. She was melting in orange flashes. Because no one could see her there . . . except maybe some flying flirt.

The next night she had a lovely time as well. The waxing and waning orange aura was tanning her even better. She sunbathed with even greater gusto, her eyelids tightly shut. Because she had locked herself out again that afternoon, and then she had the worst half hour of her life since he had left. Because the baby was locked inside . . . Hence, Pipina didn't have time to wait for some lockout service. Of all the men in the world, the only one who could have helped her in that moment was Jesus. And he did. The door to the roof was open! And from the roof Pipina lowered herself onto her balcony. And the balcony door was cracked open. Jesus is . . . Some man yelled up at her from the street, you had a 75 per cent chance of falling. He slowed her down . . . Just then the baby plopped down off the couch. Good thing she was home already. She started to picture what would have happened if she hadn't been . . . And in the morning, at the drug store, she had to leave the shampoo at the cash register. Because she didn't have enough money. She had been needing it for three days. And it was already rung up. The people in line were more anxious than the new cashier, who didn't know which way was up and had to go get the manager. One man banged his laundry detergent on the counter next to Pipina and leaned in on the other side of her, hissing right into her ear, her favourite, stupid cow, and as he was pushing his way out, he licked her whole back and butt with his belly. Her knees gave way a little, but the counter steadied her . . . So when she finally fell asleep, tormented by guilt, when she felt the top of the baby's head where it had hit the floor, she kept hearing it . . . she dreamed that someone liked her. That someone loved her. Just the way she was . . . Literally, on warm sand. And she caressed and patted it, clean and white as could be. She kept pouring a powdery waterfall in front of her face. One grain was more pink and silver than the next. As far as the eye could see . . . And not a cigarette butt in sight. He didn't smoke . . . She didn't know who, but she knew that he existed! She felt the way you do when you have a mother. When everyone's home. She was certain that someone liked her. He had to tell her. I love you. And there's nothing I can do about it. And nothing else matters, only to be together . . . Dreams were good for her. Her stomach had even stopped hurting after every meal . . .

And wherever she went, they made her wait and slammed the door in her face. Wherever she went, she had to stand in every line and got sent from one counter to another. She wasn't disabled enough for the people who were working to be ashamed in front of each other. Sipping their coffee, talking about their miserable salaries. Because the coffee will get cold, and she didn't bring a cookie. She's looking in here! So what? Is she famous? No. She can wait . . . Often referred to as she, only once in a while as that lady. She didn't encounter professional behaviour. Only excuses citing official procedure. One time, when she woke up in an overcrowded waiting room to the sound of you, you, you in the coat, you by the wall, you with the child, you, you . . . it must have been going on for a while, because everyone was looking at her, including the baby with its eyes like plums . . . it occurred to her that she should wear red. A nose! That made her smile. And the nurse's indignant face drooped with even greater, more genuine loathing. I'd love to take a nap too! And the nurse started to turn around like a tank. Get a move on, you're not the only one in here, they spawn children and . . . And then not a sound could be heard, fat blocked the doorway. Pipina got up in a flash, but she fell back on her butt even faster and patted her leg, which had fallen asleep. They had been waiting longer than usual. Finally, wincing, hissing, she limped towards the door which had been unblocked with incredible effort. Only one naughty corner of her mouth was still grinning. Because she thought about how the nurse's giant, tormented thighs couldn't fit one in front of the other. How they chafed. How she had to stuff a giant piece of dead-weight flesh into an enormous bra. And then do it all over again! How everything cut into her, pinched, how she hated summer . . . Undress it. Once again not the baby, not the patient. It . . . And Pipina struggled, the little hands and feet weren't cooperating. It was taking too long. The nurse and the doctor tore their police gazes away from them for a second and gave each other a meaningful look. Yes, everything's from a second-hand store, washed a million times but still stained, Pipina nodded, and the other corner of her mouth grinned too . . . The doctor was only two-thirds the size of the nurse, but she had also had it with summer! And Pipina tried to imagine when this doctor actually felt good. That she had a bathtub at home, filled it with nearly cold water, she knew how far so it wouldn't overflow . . . and then they all noticed a hole. It wasn't large, but it was right on the belly. On that happy little balloon. And Pipina looked straight up into the four motionless eyes and planted a kiss on the hole. She felt the soft skin, and the baby cooed like a little dove, it was ticklish . . . And Pipina knew they didn't have anything like that. The nurse, no chance, and the doctor looked like her children had left when they turned 18. Once and for all. And that morning Pipina had seen them arguing in front of the doctor's office, yeah, they had broken the waiting record that day, about who had forgotten the keys at the front desk. And the elevator hadn't been working for a week, so the nurse had to trudge up and down the stairs again. She should have studied harder. And Pipina grinned in every direction. She was imagining those thighs. A thousand times over. Good thing the huge breasts hung on one side, and the butt on the other, because balance is no laughing matter! And those poor knees that had to lift everything from one step to the next . . . That was how she started to use it. Her imagination. Like a weapon. She was quite offended by the spawned . . . and even more by the things she didn't hear . . . My dear unhelpfuls . . .

And Pipina dreamed in instalments. About a beach. And there was a toilet and a shower that worked even in wintertime. In case some madman, or hero, or both, needed them. A gleaming piece of paper was nailed to the door, and Pipina rubbed her eyes in her dream. It said that the second shower the valued guests were accustomed to had been removed to conserve water. Thank you for your understanding, and a handwritten signature of some esteemed city big shot . . . A whimper or a sigh woke Pipina up, but the baby was sleeping, stuck into the corner of its crib like a cork. And Pipina thought about our landlocked, wonky, cracked, flooded, but most of all putrid, unlockable, or on the contrary locked, public, publicly not given a damn about you-know-whats. Facilities . . . She had to take a whiff of the baby. Immerse herself in the crib atmosphere at least up to her waist. And tears came to her eyes. No one cared about them either. They were just two little drops, a shaky drop and a droplet . . . She crawled into bed, and it was almost boring. The uncertainty over whether she had forgotten something, missed something, ruined something, didn't turn something off, didn't lock something . . . When she fell asleep in the wee hours, she saw the same crescent bay. In every shade of grey. From the almost pink through pigeon, all the way to the steel spear stuck in puffed-up black storm clouds. And not a soul around, it was wintertime! Only a sign that had been posted, that somehow coasted, on shore. Warning, no lifeguard on duty today. And under the word today was a slot, and in it a piece of paper with today's date. One heck of a dream . . .

Pipina felt guilty. For walking near cars for so long. But it couldn't be helped, it was where they lived. The first tree was several streets away. Briefly she didn't understand what was going on, but then she caught on. A muscular arm, a hand blooming and closing, because it was trying to help an oncoming driver. Prey to the first cop, at first glance, because he didn't have his lights on! And Pipina knew that he was supposed to. Who knows how, year round . . . She really liked it when people helped each other, and she tried out the gesture herself. The baby could use it too, it would come in handy in the second year of preschool. It's similar to waving . . . And every day they had to say hello to the pale, sad old lady, who was all alone. I guarantee you she only cared about herself, Pipina's awful mother would have said, guaranteed . . . So Pipina coughed and said, it's quite cold today and windy too, that lady desperately needed a few words. They had known one another since, it's quite hot today and not even a leaf will budge, so the old lady said, you have to be careful around here, everything looks the same, the houses as well as the streets. And the run-down steps, and the reeking underpasses, Pipina needed to chat a bit too . . . You have to look at street names, the old lady instructed, just don't forget your glasses. Pipina nodded, and don't look at the ground. Trash and cigarette butts make everything look the same. You all look the same too. Pipina didn't understand . . . Mothers in multiyear captivity . . . And Pipina wasn't sure that she wouldn't walk on the other side of the street next time. It looked as though her awful mother had once again been right. As usual.

A day like any other went by, and she was a driver! I can only dream about that, Pipina smiled in her dream. She was an excellent driver! Who knows in what car. It was good, soft, springy! It smells like fresh sheets, she thought with delight as she drove on the highway. And someone didn't have his lights on! And Pipina knew it was mandatory, who knows how, year round. And he didn't have them on! She stuck her hand out the window, and when she thought he saw her, she opened and closed her fist like a flower. Nothing . . . So she rolled up her sleeve and tried again! She could do as many things as she needed to at the same time, she was an excellent driver. She could even whistle! But the beautiful car didn't understand, so she flashed her high beams. She even knew where her high beams were, she was a fantastic driver! But the beautiful car still didn't understand, it slowed down, and pulled in behind her. And she stuck her hand out up to her shoulder, and once again she was blooming and closing it . . . until he finally got it! He was slow on the uptake, and had a rocket-like silver car. Which at long last turned on its star-like lights, and slowly, gratefully floated by. It was so shiny that Santa could have been sitting in it. Or this smiling young man. He waved at her, and she saluted. Without smiling. Because she was unhappy that she was ugly. Because as usual, she saw the change. The one she had seen a million times before. The one that turned his relaxed, cheerful, grateful face into a polite one. She was ugly. Dream or no dream!

She walked the stroller by some big boys. And as she was going around them, the three bareheaded columns, because in her experience they wouldn't have budged an iota . . . she saw a fourth one with them. He was as short as she was. With a few colourless hairs, like she had. They were even alike in their pimples, his were burgeoning, she already had scars. The only difference was that he was completely skinny and pale. She was seeing the whole thing in slow motion, the way one does before a disaster . . . And one of those bareheaded columns said, got a cigarette?? For a second Pipina thought he was asking her. Slowly, Bratislava style. I don't, the short one said. How are you talking to me, came slowly. I don't know, in Slovak? Pipina could barely hear that brave fellow. You want me to deck you? Bratislovak is a beautiful language. He likes that sort of thing, the second column said, and Pipina remembered their reeking breaths. By then she had her back to them and was pushing the stroller up a hill, not standing still, to the rhythm of the ditty, scaredy-cat, eat a rat, say nothing and scat. This delightful little ditty emerged somewhere from her childhood. Scaredy-cat, eat a rat, say nothing and scat came in handy . . . Somewhere, as far away as possible, she sat down on a bench and was dreadfully upset that she hadn't stood up for that poor guy. Did they beat him up? She suffered like a horse. Because she hadn't so much as turned around. It may have been enough for them to notice her, she agonized. For that boy not to have been completely alone. It may have been enough for them to see that she saw them. Doing something bad. To a smaller kid. I don't smoke either, she should have said. Good thing the baby was asleep. That was why she had scrammed, so they wouldn't wake it up. Excuses, excuses, scaredy-cat, eat a rat . . . For that everything would have to be different. The whole world. Scaredy-cat, eat a rat. Well, at least half of it. Say nothing and scat. At least one country where I wouldn't be embarrassed that no one will help me, that I won't help anyone. The sun was shining . . . A tiny country where I'd want to live. A tiny homeland! It warmed them like a stove. And they slept like two tots. Mommy and baby . . . And they got a real scare when some motorcycles roared by. On a park path. Both of them cried. Sniffling, Pipina told the baby that there were good people and bad people. That you should ask them why it happened to them. And that everything human was at least half good. No, at least half bad, no, the other way around, the other way around, the other way around . . .

Sometimes she dreamed about a golf course. She had never seen it in her life. Or any other one, for that matter. Only on TV. But she knew she belonged there. I guess I can only feel good on a golf course. An abandoned one . . . And Pipina squatted and caressed the edge of the circle with fur-like grass. And with its eyes like plums the baby gaped at the hole with the flag. But . . . they weren't alone. Four men were looking at them inconspicuously. All in white. From head to toe. Two of them also had white hair, two had white hats, and one had white whiskers, a white beard, and a white hat. But none of that mattered, what mattered was the final! Pipina and the baby found themselves at the all-important, time-honoured moment when everything was at stake! The most accurate shot, the most accurate bon mot! Nonstop jokes, the gentlemen were stalling, they could barely walk any more. Fortunately, the golf cart was parked nearby. A little white car just for playing, for this specialized kind of playing. And the gentlemen were showing off and picking on each other like little boys. And Pipina was proud that the baby got to see how much they liked her. The way old gentlemen do . . . And the big moment was coming to a victorious finish, even though they had been stretching it like a garter, and the winner was exuberant, it had been worth it because we had seen it. And he waved to us. And the losers didn't want to be one-upped, after all it was just a game, and they also waved! And at least two of them felt funnier. A lot funnier! And the baby lifted its little hand and closed it twice. The first wave! One victory followed by another. And Pipina laughed out loud. The gentlemen found her enchanting. It was a nice moment in life . . . Our lives connected for ten minutes. A smile and a smile, a look and a look. We're fellow travellers, we're comrades. For a few moments, for a few years. But we take it for granted. We don't enjoy it. We're like that stupid Hitler, I want you, but you I don't even see. Or I hate you. In this world. You won't be . . . And we act like we'll be here forever. And that we'll have time to make amends for everything, catch up, apologize, learn. Golf! Step! And I'm sure we'll meet again! Because there's justice in the world . . . But for that there couldn't be any ugly girls. Like Pipina sleeping on the steps of her apartment building . . . When the cold woke her up, she started to be afraid of herself. For being so tired that some misfortune would befall them . . .

People would think me insane. If people weren't to think me insane, I'd recommend it to everyone. To let yourself be bitten by a snail. A delightful experience. Pipina remembered it from childhood . . . Back then she immediately took the snail outside, it didn't want to be there, in the stupid Mason jar. It wanted to crawl around in the summer rain. Carefully. Up periscope. One time she saw them making love. They stood leaning against one another in a bright ray of sunlight. Like a statue. Under a giant burdock leaf . . . Pipina was crazy about animals. She carried every bug, every earthworm off the road. So that they wouldn't get stepped on, run over, because the silly billlies had wandered out that way. To that inhospitable desert with no grass, no dew. Who knows where they were going?? And why didn't they turn around? They must have believed and hoped. And they weren't giving up. What did they think they'd find on the other side? A dear bug, a beloved earthworm?? Or the promised land . . . ? One time she got into a serious argument right in the forest. An old, she didn't know what to call her, told her grandson to squash something, just to be on the safe side. Some bug. In case it stings, said the, the . . . Pipina was at a loss for words. Don't you know that we come from the same branch?? Don't you know that a bigger foot will come and squash you? A small hurricane because of global warming? Either we all live or we all die. Are you the only one who has the right to this path?? Who invited you here? Do you think you belong here?? The naive one was yelling at the one who was barely swaying, like an old, rusty bridge over two worn-out high hills, not high heels! Well-worn heels sunk into the fragrant forest path . . . You don't deserve this shade! You don't deserve the meteorite that killed those poor dinosaurs, if you're the result! And to be teaching that to your grandchildren . . . Pipina really said that to her. But then she felt guilty; had it been a man, she would

89

have never dared . . . And that, that one didn't understand her anyway. And the boy was too little, completely defenceless against such stupidity. Lost, unless a miracle happened. A good teacher or a girlfriend! Because the parents must have already been infected, poisoned by that, that . . . repugnant, idiotic, rusty bridge! A person who kills a dolphin or an elephant belongs in jail. Until she's blue. Until she's green!

She paused by a shelf with children's books. I should start reading to the baby. She opened one or two, it seemed as though her awful mother hadn't thrown out a single one. And then she spotted life . . . A teeny-tiny pale animal had made its home there. It was walking around. A little clumsily, like a hippo. Except teeny tiny and transparent. Pipina waited for it to take its sweet time to walk across the page and round the corner, a page or two on . . . She hoped that those animals would get used to it, when they'd start reading. Like when people go into their forest or sea.

Try as she might, Pipina couldn't fall asleep. She kept thinking about how much money she had until the end of the month. And she didn't know what else to give up. She wanted to keep chocolate at all costs. Quartered, it gave her something to live for four times. Something to look forward to all day. Stuffing it into her mouth on the steps . . . In that land of hers, she started to call it Homeland, it wasn't embarrassing to ask how much things cost. And to look into your wallet. In that Homeland of hers no one would have rolled their eyes or thought less of you. And someone would have smiled if you had poured out all your change onto the counter. As it clinked and rolled everywhere . . . One time, back when she was little, still sheltered, and it was before Christmas to boot, a store clerk had said as they were picking it up all over the place, that's what we're here for! And Pipina remembered it forever! By then she already knew that Santa didn't bring the presents, so it was logical, imperative, that she would need one for her mother . . . And Pipina walked and walked . . . she was already very tired, her legs hurt a lot, she could barely pick them up from the snowdrifts . . . and then she thought she saw a light off in the distance . . . And the snowdrifts lay down like obedient dogs and their even more obedient shadows . . . and Pipina was standing in front of a store lit up like an altar. The store display contained everything you'd give your life for . . . She walked by twice, feigning disinterest, but then she went in. Because there were no middling women, painted to look beautiful, that look you over and write you off like men . . . There was just an old lady, and she was busy. It was a while before she mumbled, take a good look around, young lady, every other thing that looks really good on you is free . . . And in her dream Pipina thought that she must be dreaming. Who gets to be the judge of that? You, of course . . . How about a mink coat, Pipina made a feeble joke. Come on, you don't like mink coats, you love animals! That woman reminded Pipina of someone . . . I'll watch your baby. And Pipina couldn't believe her eyes, the baby really was there. Sleeping, the stroller parked by the cash register. It looks just like you. That's no good, Pipina gulped . . . We all have our feelings of inferiority as well as our dreams. Take a good look around, see if we've guessed yours. Doesn't that lady look like St Nicholas? Pipina took a deep breath, and gratefully dove into the brightness and warmth of the beautiful things . . . And minor chords sounded, and Pipina lifted her eyes and her hands off the sweaters that were as soft as the fur of young moles. The old-fashioned cash register had turned into a piano, and her grandmother, who used to live on the old square between two churches, called out as if she were singing. Pipi, your mommy called, she said good things about you, she was proud of you . . . Suddenly Pipina knew what she had needed all her life. Boots. Black, velvet, low-heeled, Catwoman boots. That would cover her ugly pointy knees . . . And the plump hands with nails like almonds played three steady, festive chords, and Pipina saw them. Thigh-high Catwoman boots . . .

They're on our bench! A couple was sitting on the practically nonexistent bench. They were so in love they would have sat on a power line. She was breathing through her mouth like a little girl, blinking about once a minute, and he talked and talked. Excuses and more excuses. Once again he hadn't said anything at home. Tears welled up in her eyes, and he had only one argument left, a kiss. It worked. It got them both. Wet, fragrant. And the goodbyes were like that too. Wet and fragrant. See you next time between the apartment buildings . . . He had planned that well, with his last bit of common sense, no one would look for them there . . . And she gracefully got into her sweet ride that was accustomed to a garage the size of a barn and honked sadly, and he headed towards another such spotless car, his head almost touching his knees. He could feel that kiss all over. He really didn't know what to do. Once again they didn't break up. Once again he'd have to make excuses and more excuses at home. A stalemate. Pipina felt sorry for him . . . She sat on the single slat that was left of the whole bench. She could never figure out what someone got out of, what the thrill was, what the satisfaction was in destroying a bench. Doing something bad?? So that no one could tie a shoelace there again? She thought about it every now and then. Every chance she got. It must be about strength. To be strong enough to destroy a bench. To beat up a guy. But what if he's small and the bench is old?? To break off the branches of a cherry tree almost at the trunk and pick the cherries afterward? To leave those used limbs strewn around with their leaves like dusty rags, which don't understand, are panting for sap, dying . . . At least there was some lazy logic in that, but it was so sad and ungrateful that she caressed, picked up, stacked those branches next to the poor tree. The stubs overhead tattled. You've made a fundamental error, you produced cherries but you're not behind a fence! If you're in a housing complex, don't produce cherries if you value your life! Ignorance is no excuse, my dear . . . Pipina sat on that bent slat, as close to the edge as possible so as to be as light as possible, and the baby slept under that poor tree that could neither run nor bite . . . And a bird flew by and she looked up. Into a giant face. Into gaping eyes. A dog was looking at her from four inches away. And Pipina didn't blink either . . . And the huge maw licked itself, a strange breath wafted over . . . another split second, or a hundred years, and the dog slowly turned around and left. It went on its way. A big, lonely mastiff. And Pipina backed up towards the baby under that poor tree, and she felt like food. But not good enough.

And at night she dreamed about rest. Grass like a mattress, cut short, springy, damp with dew . . . Everywhere. It was a huge green space. And in it, only Pipina and the sun with its green flashes. I can only feel good on a golf course. An abandoned one . . . It got dark, and she lifted her head. She saw an enormous flock of birds. The first ones were already landing nearby, less than 20 feet from her, the last ones were still blocking the sun. And the grey tongue licked the space and set down. Dozens of birds hopped around happily, even off in the distance . . . The baby won't believe me, Pipina thought in the green air. She was able to breathe in that greenery like a fish in water. Like in her Homeland.

She locked herself out again. That'll be 30 euros again. Again she was waiting and waiting for the man she had finally reached on a cell phone she had to beg to borrow. It took her two tries. The first woman kept making excuses that she didn't have one, that she couldn't lend it, that she'd get in trouble . . . But the second woman didn't say a word, she just dumped out her frightful purse by the fence and found it. Pipina had never seen such a cell phone. Taped all over. Thank you. You're welcome. And then the woman picked up all her things and left. Without a single unnecessary word or glance. She looked at Pipina once when Pipina addressed her, and a second time when Pipina said thank you . . . And then Pipina waited and nursed the baby on her favourite steps, and thought about what kind of a man she'd want to show up. If she could choose, what kind of a man should appear . . . And the baby let go like a ripe raspberry, and Pipina thought about how disappointed he'd be. Because her voice wasn't ugly. She liked talking on the phone. On the phone she was bold, she even joked around . . . What if the man who came was, let him be like the man she had passed on the stairs once. A sad, good-looking man in casual, light-coloured clothing. Hair the colour of silver sand, ruffled by the wind a little. Pipina had a thing for dark blond men, just like her awful mother. Who always pretended to be kidding . . . This one was at that age when people look the way they are, the way they live. He said something to Pipina and looked right into her eyes. He gave her the kindest smile in her current life, by a long shot. Those by women included . . . No wonder that Pipina, with all of her regular hang-ups, plus her English-language hang-ups, gave him such a confident and deaf look . . . and she bumped the stroller down two steps like it was nothing . . . all she could do was guess at what the kindest sentence in her current life by a long shot sounded like. Including those spoken by women . . . May I help you down these frightful, slippery, dangerous, big steps?? She looked over her shoulder, but he was lagging behind, looking like a lost puppy. The Englishman . . . Something so simple would have never crossed his mind, that she didn't speak English, that she had made love four times in her life, and that her complexes were even uglier than she was.

You should never lie. Her awful mother had taught her that. The one who didn't know anything. And if she did, then it was wrong! So, when you're alone, you should stay alone, and that's that?? It was Saturday, and they were going to a funeral . . . She didn't know whose, and the rest of the people didn't know that they didn't belong there. She had come up with that ploy a long time ago. It was a good lie for getting to be around people . . . Not weddings. Not even big ones! You'd feel awkward eating. And someone could ask how you're related. But at a funeral no one would ever find out where and how much your lives had crossed paths. With the deceased. And for a short time or for a long time? And long ago or recently? Who knows?? And Pipina and the baby got to be around people . . . Within arm's reach. But not like on a bus . . . And everyone was dressed in their Sunday best, they spoke in pleasant voices, exchanged looks of understanding, and the baby was the only little, sweet, for now good thing around, and the sight of it made some people feel good. For an hour they really belonged there. Pipina was still smiling when she was changing the baby that night, what a nice funeral. The funeral service was being interpreted from German. She had great legs and a beautiful mouth. And she knitted beautifully. And she laughed like a turtle dove . . . And Pipina said to herself, hats off, when she took a good look at the grumpy old woman on the photo above the casket. And she was all the more impressed when the murmurs carried to her that her son was the one speaking! But why not in Slovak? His mother would have preferred it this way, she was born in Berlin. The murmurs knew everything. And he asked, how did you know her . . . Pipina wanted to say, we were close, but instead she made a joke, she watched the stroller for me once. And the murmurs murmured that she was funny and spread the word that they had been close . . . And the organ made every good string vibrate in everyone, and outside the enormous windows it was pouring. But inside, people were warm, dry, connected by reverent thoughts. And as the casket was going down, in that quietest of quiets, the baby uttered a high-pitched cry. Like a tiny flute. And tears welled up in people's eyes, and the son together with everyone else cried like the baby. And everyone felt relief. Everyone felt better. And Pipina was proud that they had helped . . . When they got home, she actually had the feeling that they had gone somewhere, that something had happened. And she had something to remember. Saturday was no longer empty. Lying's worth it, mom. By the way, we could do that professionally.

A more remote bench! On a small bridge. Things started out well, but then they went downhill. Two old people said, have a seat, it's a nice bench, and we need to go anyway . . . The old man started to get up, I used to go for walks with our son, I used take him out in the stroller. When, the old woman said sharply, and Pipina knew there was trouble . . . You haven't taken him for a walk in your life. The man sat back down. I regularly took him for walks. You had other things on your mind. Like what? I have no idea, I'm not a Hungarian Jewish Bolshevik. And Pipina breathed a sigh of relief.

She thought the woman had changed her mind about the argument . . . I was a Bolshevik, I am still a Jew, but most importantly, I did take the baby for walks. The woman smiled. *Nekem monďa peštinek?* Pipina didn't understand a word of that . . . But you had it pretty good. Unlike many other women. The woman picked up her cane. The man was groping for his. I was nice. You were miserable. The woman's cane struck the ground. Why didn't you divorce me? The man grabbed a bag handle. My parents would have been ashamed. The woman grabbed the other handle. I was starting to worry you weren't going to mention them. The man and the woman stood up. They did warn me. And they ruined my life. They set off . . . Neither of them had raised their voice even once. And the woman matched his step, left and left, they were disappearing . . . They didn't even wave bye to Pipina and the baby. For one, they didn't have a free hand, and for another, Pipina and the baby were just a drop and a droplet in their sea of arguing . . . And then some Bratislava natives and a policeman appeared under the bench. Each from a different direction. Pipina actually went, yikes. She should have known that such a bench would come at a price. Too much went on there! And on top of it all, the pacifier fell. The baby spat it out, Pipina tried to catch it, but the pacifier bounced off her hand and it was falling, falling, all the way under the bridge . . . And the policeman said, boys, hand the lady that pacifier. And the scariest one of them brought it to her, here you are, and he was holding it by the ring. Don't worry, it was in the grass. It caught Pipina so off guard that she just nodded abruptly, but she still licked it . . . And then the policeman came over and sat down. Is a policeman allowed to do that?? And he spoke to the baby. And he joked, that the baby wasn't answering, that it was busy with its pacifier. Once again she wasn't important, but he was very polite, and he said he wouldn't leave without a goodbye wave. That without a wave he wouldn't take a step, he wouldn't go on duty. And the baby waved. Either by chance, or it got scared like Pipina . . . And then a neighbour walked by, saying, I'm keeping an eye out for the mailman, because he'll toss a slip in my mailbox again, and I'll have to go to the post office. If you'd like, I'll walk the stroller for you for 15 minutes, so I'm not just standing around . . . Mailmen these days, Pipina said, and she dashed off as fast as her feet would carry her. Wherever she wanted to . . . for seven and a half minutes.

They were standing in line again. Pipina felt like she spent half of her life in lines. This time it was at the post office. The mailman had tossed a slip into her mailbox, even though she was at home . . . It was a particularly overworked, shabby post office. Pipina had yet to get lucky and find an open service counter when she showed up. All post offices are alike, her awful mother said once. I feel like I could be anywhere in the world! Her mother stood in a queue, her awful mother used to say in a queue. And little Pipi wrote invisible messages in invisible ink on visible pieces of paper. And she folded them to be as little as possible, and when no one was looking, she stuck them into some secret crack. Old creaky writing stands had tons of them. First a letter to Santa, then an appeal for that which had been broken and was hidden behind a flower pot to be whole again, for that which had been lied about and would be reported to be forgotten, and couldn't she be as pretty as Kristína from her class. And she'd like a mother like Kristína's too. One who didn't say such awful things . . . Airports and train stations are all alike too, you could be anywhere at one of those, couldn't you? Her awful mother had just said, but no one answered. And bathrooms, they're also all alike, aren't they? That's another place we could be anywhere. Her mother talked to strangers, everywhere and always. I wonder whether that applies to our putrid and pissed-all-over ones! Her mother really said putrid and pissed-all-over, and people snickered, and Pipina was embarrassed, even though it was true . . . They had been in many bathrooms, and all of them were frightening. Except at home. Kristína's mother definitely didn't say such things, things that others don't say. And in a queue of all places!

Pipi, you're a pity. It rhymed nicely and it had the right rhythm. Pipina went uphill, pushing the stroller with all her will. She was going there again . . . Right at the back of the bus stop, the back of the bus shack, there was a green gate. A not-so-large, old, stone gate overgrown by wild roses, with a dark green shadow in the middle. The people nervous about why isn't it here yet, why is it running late again, didn't even notice it. But Pipina actually looked forward to it . . . The first time she had gone in, she pulled the stroller behind herself as a precaution. Until the shade of every kind of leaf and leaflet parted into a mist, and Pipina saw a cheery, light green lawn with two nice benches. A light breeze danced on the lawn, and a little brass plaque gleamed on each bench. Tomáš used to sit here, Táňa used to sit here. The Maštalírs wish you a pleasant stay . . . Maybe they had a house here, while they needed one. And then, who knows whether it was Tomáš's idea or Táňa's, they gifted this place to everyone. For relaxation. All you had to do was bring something to drink. An old gentleman brought the food . . . In the middle of the lawn stood a thin gentleman in a hat and a dark, long, winter coat. In front of him were birds in several rows, like a choir. Blackbirds and thrushes were on tiptoe, stretching their necks. Even a few crows that were a head taller lined up. They didn't look menacing though. Only a few young sparrows couldn't sit still, but they weren't brave enough to set down on the ground. And the gentleman, a slice of bread in hand, pinched off little pieces and tossed them with a single precise movement, as if he were pointing, you, now you, now it's your turn, now yours, watch out. And the appropriate bird went chomp and gulp and went back to watching him. The old gentleman was fair, conducting even the ones in the back. No one was fighting, no one was stealing, a chirp could only be heard every now and then, it was an eating orchestra . . . There was one bird the conductor didn't notice, it was right under his feet. So the bird left . . . It turned its head once, by 15 degrees, and off it went. To the green wall. There it hopped up and flew away. And Pipina had her first good laugh in a long time. But the gentleman didn't turn around, he was used to an audience . . . They went there at least twice a week, like to a concert. It made her feel like she was in Vienna, or in Homeland.

Pipina knew she shouldn't, but she did anyway. She took a whiff. Of the cologne he had forgotten there! The one she had been walking by in the entryway, ready in case he came back for it. The one whose loss he had accepted, the one he had given up on, the one he preferred to write off half-full . . . And Pipina spent half the day whimpering, everywhere she went, like a sick dog. She tried to stop, the baby started to imitate her, but she couldn't help herself, she would have exploded. She missed him so badly. It had been so beautiful. He smelled so good . . . She didn't wash it off until it was time for their afternoon walk, but that reminded her that she didn't have anything for dinner. She was still nursing, and he was gone, so she kept forgetting. Tears welled up in her eyes again. Because it had been so beautiful when there was a chance he could come home. Any minute. A miracle could happen at any moment. It could appear, just one smile to make my life worth living, a little dream to build my world upon . . . She was standing at a crosswalk. On a street. Until a waiting car honked, and Pipina looked at the driver. He didn't look angry, only confused. And then she had an idea. Then she thought, he'll come . . . Anyone I want . . . You too, driver . . . I can cuddle up to anyone I want, I won't bother asking you, driver. At night . . . Everyone's asleep at night. They're available . . . And Pipina crossed the street with a smile, and the driver behind her back was still confused, until he got honked at. Everyone's available at night, even the best ones who don't swear . . . Even though they've been toiling through life for some time, they're still generous, calm, kind, a joke here and there, an idea every now and then. Pipina had excellent taste . . . Standing up straight. Hard to the touch. Always curious. But not about women. Enthusiastic, but not about women. And at night they could be hers . . . All of them . . . At night I can hold hands with that Englishman, if I want to. When he's asleep . . . If he happens to dream about it, he'll forget it in the morning. If anything, in the morning they'll forget. A stupid dream . . . And Pipina carefully crossed another street, because beware, the cat must take care, and she stood on the sidewalk again. Theoretically, someone could marry me at night. Make me his wife. It's dark. And adopt the baby. The baby's good when it's asleep. And in the morning, no memory of any of it. No problem, I'm used to it, we're used to it . . . Someone walked by, and Pipina howled. Like an old, sick, hungry dog. She got a whiff of his scent . . . He won't come back even for a nearly full . . .

I can dream about anyone I want! I could walk around holding hands with Milan Lasica! Let's say, around Bratislava castle! Her awful mother had said that it only had the outer walls, floors, and towers with no roofs. And every floor was hollow. It was just a giant overturned stone table with shelves. Three, four of them? In the whistling wind, around the huge empty windows, I'll be very careful, always holding hands, walking around with my reserved Lasica. Just so, willy-nilly. Hither and thither. Because he's got a clue. He knows my awful mother's vocabulary. He knows what a *firhang* is, and what are *francle*. And a *štokerlík* and a *hokerlík*, and a *fijók* and a *šuflík*, and all those *pakšaméty*. Including *zicherajsky*. And don't think I'm lionizing, I'm just improvising . . . And it's done and dusted. Pipina seldom watched TV, only once in a blue moon, but what if he really was like that. Not too cheerful, but sure footed. More or less. Already. Good. Still . . . No doubt he knows what a *karperecka* is . . . When I close my eyes, I can be wherever I want, with whomever I want, and *fertig*. And it's no skin off my nose. And don't run around in that *lapítka,* missy. Pipina covered herself with her bathrobe . . . And as her muscles and tendons were relaxing, she felt a smile spread across her face. And she felt like a boy playing hookie . . .

Pipina never took the baby into bathrooms. The same way she never sat down on a toilet seat anywhere but at home. Not that she was following her awful mother's advice, for whom that was rule number one . . . They were at the hospital, so she asked the closest nurse to watch the stroller for a moment, because she had to go to the restroom. The nurse looked as though she had swallowed a fly, she gave a big sigh . . . but Pipina had no choice any more and rushed in. And when she bent over, bowed down, she saw the tiles up close. They were clean. They smelled good. They smelled good?? She looked around in disbelief, there was toilet paper, a trash can, yet there was no sign, place your used feminine products in the trash, without a please, without a thank you. She took another whiff, it was clean in there! She got dressed, walked out to the sinks, saw herself. Wrinkled, tired. She bowed her head and caught a whiff of a stench. Her own. She also saw her dirty shoes, they had come on foot, in lieu of a walk. She looked up, there were worn out, yellowed sinks all around, and bad feminine odour. Everything was as usual, and she hurried to protect herself as best as she could. And she wondered, but we're at a hospital . . . Pipina had nothing to dry her hands on, so she went back for toilet paper. She opened the door like a surgeon, like her awful mother, with her elbows and her shoulders. And a ray of sunlight half closed her eyes with its warmth, and something was different. A scent! The good smell was back. And everything was clean, shiny, white! Pipina turned around and dashed, she didn't even pay attention to how she was touching the door handles . . . She only recovered once she came face to face with the annoyed nurse. Thank you, she hung her gaze into the stroller. And post offices and airports are alike too!! You could be anywhere at one of those!!

On their afternoon walk Pipina was grossed out. It was already Wednesday, and the trash hadn't been picked up yet. And the wide-open, broken dumpsters were practically half empty. It had been a really windy night . . . Even when it wasn't windy, and the trash truck was in the right place at the right time, it was nothing to write home about. Maybe when people toss an apple core behind themselves like a shot glass or they flick a cigarette butt off their

103

balcony, it makes them feel free or rich for a second. But when the wind runs amok, oh . . . That was how bad her mood was. The baby was sleeping, and Pipina wanted to as well. She was sitting on their one-slat bench under the stupid cherry tree. And just as her eyelids were closing, she spotted a narrow passageway between the apartment buildings. Just a small gap, a little wider than the stroller. What kind of a shortcut is that? She got up. It had never been there before. Where does that crummy gapola lead? She peeked in. Light called from up ahead . . . And then she couldn't go forward or back for a moment. It would be hard to imagine such a combination, such a collection of the most basic, most disgusting things in various stages of decay, let alone walk on it. It was moving, she felt like throwing up. But what if we have to go back this way. And there was a fresh breeze, and the light got brighter, and they stumbled over the last pad right onto an emerald. Onto a crew cut lawn. Onto a golf course. A hundred times better than on TV, they weren't far from those big sand teardrops! At a housing complex?? Pipina looked at the dark gap behind her. A toilet?? For dogs and the homeless?? The more putrid the better?? Her knuckles had turned white on the stroller handle . . . Slowly they walked a few feet. It was easy as pie on the perfectly manicured grass. They were cleaning their feet, wheels, lungs . . . Could we be anywhere?? When time and space create a knot? Is golf the sport of my Homeland?

Summer! Who needs trousers, who needs panties, on the beautiful, sun-bleached seashore?? She took off her panties, and it was darn good luck that no one from the whole wide housing complex was looking. And that she had left her shoes on, even though she was walking on sand . . . For weeks she had been relentlessly sorting trash. Even though the recycling bins were a few streets away. And she kept asking the city to put some closer. They were sick of her! And she kept bothering them to pick up the trash when they were supposed to. She kept checking on it and reporting it! They had had just about enough of her! And she watched the weather forecast, so she knew not only when it was going to rain, but also when it was going to be windy, and she went and closed them. The dumpsters. She had already bought herself a shovel for winter. So that she could clear the snow around them. So that they couldn't make excuses about not being able to get to them. The garbage men. And she made sure that people who weren't from her street didn't bring their trash there. Because we're paying for it, and then ours doesn't fit. Over my dead body, she'd say with a smile. And the people she had embarrassed started to spread the word that she was crazy.

And it was hot. Her awful mother used to say, sweltering! Wild horses couldn't have gotten her to the hospital, but she found an official notice in her mailbox that they had missed an immunization . . . By the time they got there, she had to go to the toilet, the hospital was far. Luckily, two nurses were chitchatting in front of the door, and they said just a moment, but they never came back . . . So Pipina pushed the stroller through the narrow doorway into the bathroom foyer. It was the usual, just stinkier, because it was summer! And Pipina turned around, better wait 'til we're home, hold it. But as she was turning around in that narrow space, a ray of sunlight struck her leg. It was warm, so she looked back. And she froze in a strange pose. Something was different! A bare foot was sticking out of the sandal. And Pipina gasped, a completely bare foot! With no hair. She closed her eyes. He was still home the last time she had shaved . . . She put her feet together and looked. She was standing on a very suspicious streak. Both legs had hair, one next to the other, one right on top of the other. What nonsense . . . But she didn't try it again. Not on your life. The inoculation, however, slipped her mind like death . . .

Pipina couldn't believe her own dream. There was the smell of water. Somewhere it was babbling, somewhere it was dripping, somewhere it was just softly, lazily reflecting, softly, lazily winding its way over giant leaves, over long grasses. And it dripped in large, rainbow drops. Because there were rainbows everywhere, including in the corners . . . And a warm fog was setting down into a dale. And fountains bloomed like flowers on a large scale. Or like huge trees, or shrubs . . . And out flowed rivulets, streamlets, or just water bogs for cute little frogs. And a very thin, three-legged dog was running by . . . It was barking happily, laughing, because it had sniffed out Homeland . . .

She told the baby about it. The baby shook its head, no-no. And Pipina said, why not?? It could be anywhere where people have the wit to know that they sit . . . on the same branch as, for example, little lizards. Where it's not being cut out from under everyone! Already as an infant the baby understood everything in the world . . . And Pipina told the baby how her awful mother had saved a flailing mole from a concrete ditch next to their garden. Who knows how long the poor thing had been trying to burrow there . . . When she heedlessly lobbed it over the fence, the wide-eyed mole, whimpering from fear, continued on with a perfectly shallow dive into the dirt. For a moment it churned the dirt, and then it submerged. A mole is one of us too! And there was one other thing the baby knew already as an infant. That champagne corks which floated up on shore were some of the cleanest things in the world. And the baby looked forward to them . . .

In the morning a sullen young man walked out of her neighbour's apartment. One sleeve almost on, the other whipping in the wind. In his haste he didn't know which way was out, how to get away, which direction were the stairs. He actually let them lead for a while, then he passed them, and vroom, he galloped off. He didn't look like he ever wanted to come back . . . But a few days later she thought she saw him on the street next to the store. It was morning; they had gone grocery shopping. He ran out of the building, yesterday's useless tie flapping wildly. He stopped, rolled it up, everything's different in the dark. And truth be told, that wasn't where his mind had been yesterday. He turned back towards the building, it was him, the same guy. He must have needed to be close to someone. Children can't fall asleep without that. And then we pretend that we've outgrown it. She felt sorry for him. And for herself . . . Come here, you're tired. Pipina turned around. She thought the boy in front of the garage was alone! We've had it, haven't we, the boy said like an adult, and picked up a ball in his arms. And Pipina thought, there are attentive, sensitive men in the world. I've forgiven you, he added, and Pipina's ears perked up. For missing. Twice! The third time you hit a post, you were trying. I know you were trying. And Pipina raised her nothing-to-speak-of eyebrows, miserable hair, miserable nails, everything's connected . . . he's making excuses, like the rest of them . . . And a pitiful, old, shaky man struggled to get into a car. She didn't know whether to help or avert her eyes. Great music came on. He turned on some great jazz. And Pipina stalled, stepping from one foot to the other, until she heard it! Rock 'n' roll . . . And a skateboarder, whom she had heard from afar so she had pushed the stroller up to the fence, zoomed by, and he stopped so hard that sparks flew, picked up a rumpled-up newspaper, and whizzing by the dumpster, he tossed it in. 7–0, he shouted . . . And a tall man who was backing up bumped into Pipina who had been standing with her back to him. And both of them turned around, pardon me, pardon me, but he was already smiling at someone behind her. While still towering over her. Really close. Open mouth, strong teeth. And he was breathing . . . And it was getting dark, they should have been home already, and a little blond boy was lying on a bench at the bus stop, taking one photo after another. What else! Of it getting dark . . .

And Pipina was turning into a libertine. One day she dreamed about one man, the next day about another. She bloomed all of them into a dream. Used them to the last drop. They loved her. At least platonically. They were fantastic. And she kept changing things up. Your dream is my command! And Pipina started to feel wonderful. Like an outlaw. And she couldn't choose. The guiltier she felt, the more she fell in love with each of them, to make up for what they had no idea about. It was so exhausting, she actually lost weight! A regular beast! In her dreams she was so relaxed that at any moment a conversation could turn into a kiss . . .

Once again they were trudging to the hospital. They couldn't get out of that immunization! On the way they took out the trash, and Pipina was wiping her hands on the grass. As usual, the dumpster was foaming with plastic bags like a beer mug, and Pipina's hands had sunk into it. Why don't people tie them up better! They can't leave them outside, the garbage men won't pick them up, it's not their job, their job's the dumpster! Yuck! And as Pipina thought about going back home to wash her hands, she bumped into another floating stuffed plastic bag. I'm sorry . . . Her ears perked up, the woman sounded like she was crying, do you need help? Nothing can help me! Pipina got really scared, did something happen to you?? Can't you see? No. Are you blind?? Pipina stared at the woman with her little eyes. Little eyes, big ears, everything's connected. No! I have a terrible haircut! I look like a department store clerk! And Pipina finally understood. It's not that bad. Yes it is, the woman got angry. The same thing happened to me years ago, they did the same kind of a bob! And no amount of crying will fix it, Pipina finally produced the correct response. No amount of bawling will fix it, the woman nodded her bobbed, robbed, though still flat head . . . And Pipina went on her way, shaking hers, which not even a hood would help, take care! Easy for you to say! I know . . . And at the doctor's office a man was subbing in for their usual doctor. The flu was to blame. And the word was that he didn't even have a nurse. She couldn't fit through the front door any more, Pipina thought, and then things picked up speed. A lovely bass spoke her name. The doctor was calling the patients himself. And Pipina was pulling the baby out of the stroller in a hurry, and the baby was crying, and everything was falling out of Pipina's terribly stinky hands. They should have gone back! But that robbed bobbed woman had gotten Pipina all mixed up . . . You've got it so good, your mommy's so talented, what's your name? And Pipina stammered so much that she looked like an idiot, and she couldn't get the baby's chubby leg out of the onesie. It's stuck! The baby won't let me! May I?? Here we go . . . And the doctor did everything that needed to be done, he even put the onesie back on the baby, and the baby screamed in his face the whole time. Teeny-tiny vocal cords vibrated in the gaping red mouth. Pipina had never seen or heard anything like it. She couldn't ask him anything. She couldn't bring herself to look him in the eye. When they walked out . . . she had to sit down. She slumped, pushed her way in between all the people on the bench, flu or no flu. And the door clicked, and the bass said, excuse me, is she still here . . . and he spotted her, came over, and placed all the things she had forgotten in her lap. She had forgotten everything. What I wouldn't give for such a mommy. He felt very sorry for the baby, but he didn't so much as flinch. Only his jaw quivered righteously . . . But she didn't see it, she didn't lift her head until after the door clicked again. And by the time they packed up, by the time they got out of the way, she dropped everything twenty times over. And as she was picking things up twenty times over, the sign on the door inscribed itself in her memory twenty times over: Dr Norbert Fuxberger . . .

His life was a failure. It was almost a foregone conclusion. He had failed at the most important thing, not being alone . . . His son came up with that . . . Whenever someone did something abhorrent or unjust, at work, on TV, in history, and nothing happened to him, he didn't pay the price . . . his son would declare, he'll be alone in his old age! It lessened the injustice, it put the world back to right, it gave life logic . . . He and his wife had divorced long ago. The lottery didn't work out. So he devoted himself to his job. He was good at it. His son he lost recently. The son got married. He didn't understand it. Not why his son got married, but why he had been alone since then. A heart has room for many loves, much love . . . Not that he liked his daughter-in-law very much, like every good parent he felt that his son was fit for a royal court. Fairy tale included. Because his son was good . . . She mostly wanted to have a good time. He thought. She had forgotten about fairy tales long ago. He thought. She didn't help his son much. He thought. When they were getting to know one another, she lied, body and soul. He thought . . . To him too. You have such a beautiful relationship, she said. I'll never get between the two of you, she said. He didn't understand what she was talking about, so he smiled.

A dream like a dream. Pipina received a bouquet. The first one in her life. She had even had to buy her own wedding bouquet. And the scent rose up to her nose like steam. Visible, unfamiliar. The bouquet blossomed right in front of her eyes. A crimson ball opened into large, fat petals. When they landed in place, there was a velvety snap. Then, one by one, the petals popped, and each time Pipina got pleasantly startled. Deep green beaks crawled out of the petals. As if they were bird heads, as if they were alive. Three from each petal. They looked around and bloomed into crimson lilies. Emerald green pollen glistened on large black filaments, and in the middle was a super long, twisted pistil. As usual, it was gold . . . Pipina couldn't come to her senses. Intoxicated, she let her hands drop and saw the bouquet from the side. Perfectly arranged from a single stem. And on a note tied with a ribbon it said: Dr Norbert Fuxberger.

His son told him that he was ruining the atmosphere. That he was ruining everything for everyone . . . The first sentence could have been true at that moment, the second one he didn't understand at all. Since everything was new, since everyone was just figuring things out. Being together. Being close. In different ways. Working together in different ways. They had their whole lives to figure it out. To become friends, to come to understand one another . . . He and his son were lifelong companions, she was the add-on, the third. Since they could remember, they had always turned the plates upside down, so that they'd drip dry. It was logical, let them drip dry, he dared say. And she got mad. But he wasn't the one who was supposed to be wearing rose-coloured glasses, he wasn't the one who would get caressed at night and everything would go back to right. He wasn't the one freshly in love . . . This was their household, and the plates would be stacked the way she wanted. Not the way they drip dry?? She was not his cup of tea. But he wasn't the one marrying her. And they had plenty of time . . . But soon his son had the same surly voice. And an expression unlike any he had known. And a little while longer, and it wasn't just the dishes that were getting stacked differently, everything was different. Even the past had been re-evaluated. It was reminiscent of socialist history . . . That which didn't fit got crossed out. They were no longer the pleasant, loving, safe, generous times. With their own language. This pwate's for pway. To be remembered time and again. I heard you have lice in preschool. They want to live too! Touching every time they passed by each other, at least with a glance. I'll loll over again! With a million nicknames and long-forgotten reasons for them. Now he was just Father. Even his picture, which had accompanied his son on all his studies, had disappeared off the secretary, he must have been done studying . . . Do you know what that was? A protectorate! You always did what you wanted, everything always had to be your way. All of a sudden it looked so lame. But I was the one responsible. It pretty much had to be the way I pretty much knew how. A person has no other gauge! No knee-high socks on the first day of school, it's cold. The fact that it ended up not being quite so cold, now he had to pay for that. God knows why it suited you . . . He certainly made mistakes. We all drive, but only Loprais wins the Dakar Rally. But he was sure that he had always valued, loved, and respected his son the same, no matter whether he was half an inch or six feet tall. And that he had never hesitated. They don't want to play with me! She doesn't love me! He always felt it was an honour to jump into the fray with a lump in his throat . . . His whole life he had pretty much told the truth. To his son as well, albeit a small, children's version. But when he wasn't excited about the plates being right side up, now that was another story . . . now he was the enemy. Eccentric, untrustworthy, inadequate in every way. His whole life. Everyone helps his children but you. You don't have anything. I liked my work. That's what I'm talking about, you never made any money. I made enough to take us on vacations. Everyone was stunned that I spent them with you . . . No one planned anything with him any more. But you don't ski. And you did? Only the unavoidable, the latest thing no one was looking forward to, Christmas was all they had left . . . Always amazing, just like when he was little! And like when his son was little! And getting better all the time, because then proud Santa brought something new for the adults too . . . He was able to say Our Father.

A dream like two dreams! A pair of earrings. Loops. With hummingbirds! Supposedly, in the olden days they used to chain them by the leg. Nowadays, it's enough to put the earrings on, open the little cage, and talk to them, or to yourself, or sing, and they flit over. They're very curious. They fly around your face a few times and get to know you. But don't close your eyes! Have you ever seen jewellery fly? A few days later you can even go out. They're like little dogs. Once in a while something attracts their attention, but soon they're back. All you have to do is whistle. Gently, like when you don't know how. They won't tell. They're the most tactful birds in the world. They only gossip amongst themselves. But their little beaks never close! Watch out for wind though, they're too light. Basically, when you don't need a hat, it's good for them too, they'll be very happy. They'll look very good on you. All you need is to have some flowers at home. A few specks of pollen, a dew drop . . . One could be called Brilliant and the other Diamond. Nicknamed, Flash and Dash! suggested Dr Norbert Fuxberger.

What would you like for dinner? Pasta? The daughter-in-law asked his son tenderly. Yes, yes! Pasta? Yes, yes, yes! Pasta? More than anything! But this needs to be eaten. I don't feel like eating this, I feel like pasta. But this needs to be eaten. But . . . And then the daughter-in-law fed his son, and his son was in seventh heaven . . . They got quiet every time he walked into the room. Then they struggled to restart the stalled conversation. And they whispered, or they'd leave it until they were in the car, I'll tell you later. Previously unheard of at their house . . . They rolled their eyes, shook their heads, as if he were a misbehaving child. You made a mistake! I just forgot. And now you're blaming others! I just thought you were going that way. You did something wrong and now you're trying to extort. Extort? That was a strange, non-family word . . . He whispered a couple of times too, he had only known her for a short time, he was embarrassed in front of her. But his son snapped at him immediately, it's not polite to whisper. And what are you going on about?? What am I going on about? He felt like they were talking about someone else, and he was sincerely sorry for that person. Just that we've been through a lot together. I've been gone for years! But we wrote each other every day, we called. I had to do everything by myself. I was always there for you. Only when you missed me, not when I needed you. At least I always prayed my funny little prayer for you. You're always talking about yourself. That brought on a wave of nausea. You're always saying the same things . . . Sometimes he tried to participate in a conversation, what did they tell you, who called? Are you snooping?? Followed by an indignant stare. He didn't know his son was capable of such. No, I just want to know how you're doing, the both of you, he clarified . . . He decided to stop calling. Except once in a while, when he forgot, when he was having a really hard time. For one, they put him on speakerphone, so not a sound could be uttered privately, and for another, only half participated. He always said the same thing as usual, the old, familiar, natural creed, but the answer was just yes, yes. His son never said any more, me too, you're mine too. We're with you, be with us. Those tender words never again fell like dew on an ordinary, parched day. That funny, time-honoured tenderness for children on the everyday, adult wading through reality. Only yes, yes . . . Those little words they had invented together must have belonged to a new love now. And the tone was meant for him to finally realize it. Bye, then . . . But this wasn't supposed to be a business call. But a business call wouldn't make you sad . . .

Pipina was a virtuoso of dreams. She saw huge, round, green hills, connected by narrow, round, green valleys. Inside them were nestled boulders flat as skipping stones, but huge. They couldn't be skipped . . . But if you ball up, if a stone slides you to the middle . . . you feel like you're in god's basket. Like you're in your mother's warm embrace. Like you're in a million-year-old embrace of the earth. Like you're at the centre of the universe. You're lying . . . giving in, resting among the suns and the planets . . . Where we belong. Together. Said Dr Norbert Fuxberger.

And he didn't know what to do about it, because he had a habit. Because there is a huge difference between the most reliable, the dearest, the surest of sure things, and someone undereducated, underinformed, imprecise, unsuccessful. Annoying. Through his own fault, by his own nature. No one likes you. The summary, just in case. What about you . . . he couldn't get it across his lips, you used to. I was little. And when you were big? I was tactful . . . He was no longer even that funny leeward side for a rest, for putting your feet up, for watching movies together, he and his son no longer knew how to talk to one another . . . Not to mention joke or fantasize. Just like when one has stage fright. And they felt awkward, even when it was just the two of them, they were honest people . . . Can't you read? What's taking you so long? You call that parking? How come you don't know something so simple? That was how short their conversations had become. His son didn't need to know anything about him any more . . . Perhaps a joke would have been good. But nothing funny occurred to him in that danger zone. With every passing day he was losing the natural sense of happiness, unchanged since his son's birth. A wave of happiness, the bigger the older his son got, didn't wash over him any more every time he thought about him. Joy no longer blossomed in his heart because he was always with him . . . Because he no longer saw the flicker of delight in his son's eyes, the spark of happiness, just because they met. Because they were together! That uncontrollable little flash that gives meaning to life. His son wasn't happy that he had come. He didn't even get up, they didn't get up, you see we're eating. He was interrupting. He was an obligation, a burden, he was . . . I have no choice, and what is that man wearing again . . . He had lost the immunity of a beloved person. He was getting on his son's nerves now . . . We all have our faults. But our loved ones have lovely ones.

Pipina dreamed about a town. An unfamiliar, extraordinary town. Dark, shiny sidewalks, at first she thought they were wet, carefully sloping into streets. Crosswalks with bright white stripes, just like on a Beatles cover. She felt like she could meet them. Freshly trimmed trees, cut in new city fashion, each with its rain platter.

Streetlights like giant snowdrops were just coming on. Warm light scattered far and wide, it was dusk . . . But Pipina had no idea where she was, where they were. People were dressed up, they had washed hair, they were laughing, old and young alike, but Pipina didn't know why. She understood the laughter, but not the language. They must have wandered around there for a long time, she was tired . . . There was a gust of wind, and people turned their heads in surprise, and the wind came back and fixed their hair. And everyone laughed again. But Pipina was cold, she put her arms around herself, it was a north wind. Then all of a sudden everything turned purple, and Pipina was standing under the neon sign of Hotel California. Exhausted. It could have been the north wind that pushed her in and closed the door behind her. Instantly it was warm, quiet, pleasant . . . But there were mirrors everywhere. She wasn't just ugly, she was also dirty. Unhappy, she half-closed her eyes, but by then they were asking her, how can we be of service. Pardon me? Pipina didn't understand. What can we do for you? Probably. And Pipina had to clear her throat, a room, please . . . This time they didn't understand. I'd like to get a room. They weren't catching on, they kept blinking. And Pipina bent down for her weapon, the baby. It weighed a ton, it woke up, she woke it up, it whimpered. They didn't like it, they found it inconvenient, it was out of place there, they shook their heads. But she couldn't imagine going back out into the wind. She got angry, lifted her free arm, pointed all around her, excuse me, is this not a hotel?? Isn't it? They shrugged their shoulders. And Pipina put her arm down, she stank. The way only she could. And they were smiling at one another, there was nothing to be done. Then they looked away . . . and back, and away . . . and she turned to follow their gazes . . . A man was standing in a frightfully tall door . . . He was tall as all . . . He greeted them, and everyone behind the desk stood up straight and smiled. And he walked in, accompanied by a pink south wind. As he walked by, he picked up the baby that was draped on her arms, and the people behind the desk were falling all over themselves, what a cute little thing . . . And he swayed gently with the baby to music, which must have floated in on the wings of that south wind, and a happy spin occurred to him, he added another one in the opposite direction, and the baby liked it and laughed . . . It was the first loud, bright laugh of the baby's life. Now the baby was someone, it knew how to laugh . . . Pipina was very proud, and she looked defiantly into the nearest mirror. And her porcine eyes turned into snail eyes, she didn't look yellow, or grey, she looked white. And they weren't coming, they were going. And the baby wasn't laughing, it was sleeping in her arms. She looked around, they were alone . . . The only reason she didn't faint was because she was holding the baby, because beware, the cat must take care. And those hateful people had hateful looks, and she pulled her wallet out of her bag with one hand and counted out money on the reception desk. And she had less and less . . . And the baby was so heavy that her knees were buckling. And the hand that kept counting the money over and over again on the reception desk shook comically. And there was nothing Pipina could do about it. It's already been paid, resounded through the hall . . . And he was coming over and bringing her water. He was spilling. But not on purpose. And they said, welcome, welcome, Dr Norbert Fuxberger.

It was as unexpected as a natural disaster. Because he had a habit. Because he was used to looking at everything pretty through four eyes. For example, at all kinds of little baubles. He had always done it that way, it was part of an education, a naive one. His son said it was gravity-fed education, all that nonsense! He had no one to tell it to any more. Come to think of it, there wasn't much to say, the world had gone out. You're just always unhappy. It was true. He was sad too . . . Do you know why you never took me to children's events? Never?? Because you would have been bored! Were we ever bored together?? You didn't sign me up for the model building club either, and everyone went to that. I thought you had your hands full. Your head full of good things. All you ever cared about was yourself. Perhaps, but we were my I . . . And do you know that you might be malicious? That really caught him off guard. And it scared him. Do you know how much she was looking forward to you?? He had no idea . . . But that he had wanted, needed, that he had missed a feminine touch somewhere nearby, close at hand, that was certain. Yet he was almost afraid of her. The same way we're afraid of the incomprehensible. Which does things we would never do . . . Everyone's supposed to have a place. If one loses it and is just being tolerated somewhere, because a father is useful once in awhile, for example once he's a grandfather . . . He almost felt like he wouldn't want to be old at his son's. He no longer felt that it was an unshakeable friendship, no matter what happened. Whatever was supposed to happen . . . He no longer felt that his son would be happy for the time they'd get to spend together. That he'd enjoy it. That he wouldn't look at his watch the whole time. He'd just be strict, yet fair. Do you know much work I've got?? I have a sense of it. You couldn't even begin to have a sense of it!! It was best not to say anything any more. And certainly not whatever came to his mind. Who's supposed to take you seriously when you say things like that?? But I'm at home. He no longer knew anything worthy of respect, worthy of remembrance, different than anyone else. It was all stale, neither here nor there, mediocre. They were no longer going through their day together, each on his side of town, of life. He was alone from his son. He had nothing to look forward to. But you love your children the way you breathe. And when you can't get air . . . Adulthood is when you notice all the things that are more interesting and smarter than your dad. But little ones are trouble too. I'll pay it back to my son! It's not about payback!! It's about ordinary togetherness. Vanished kindness. Until now he didn't know that it was kindness. The pleasant tone, the private way whenever wherever, when things were bad, when things were good, always on the same side of the barricade, thinking alike. Until now he didn't know they were on the same side. It was so automatic that the whole world was their side. It was as important as a lullaby used to be long ago . . . Now he was, now he was out there somewhere, alone. Defenceless. Like everyone who loves someone. Unhappy, because his son was unhappy that he couldn't talk to him about his love. He didn't even know why he couldn't . . . And when he woke up in the wee hours of the morning, it didn't matter whose fault it was or whether someone was to blame. It just was. There was nothing more to lose. There was nothing to be done about it. Only to wake up early in the morning to the fact that everything was out of order. And to toss and turn about it bitterly for two or three hours . . . When the alarm woke him up from his tortured sleep, the first thing that crossed his mind was, you're alone. You're a bad person.

And Pipina only dreamed about him any more! He was standing . . . It was hard to say whether on a ship, on a tower, or on a beach. Somewhere really windy. A warm wind. He was wearing a shirt and trousers, and probably nothing else. And it was becoming easier to see. First the capricious wind whipped off his collar, then the third and fourth buttons were slowly but surely losing strength. The shoes he had kicked off himself, he was enjoying having his throat caressed, his stomach, he found it funny. He opened his mouth wider to be able to taste the wind, and he lifted his arms and gave in, and the shirt flew off, and he followed . . . And Pipina shaded her eyes with both hands to be able to see him as long as possible. How he was doing in seventh heaven. Dr Norbert Fuxberger!

Birds of a feather flock together. Whenever he walked out of the building, he waved a little. Surely they weren't looking, why would they have been looking, but old habits die hard. And until he reached the corner, he wondered whether he hadn't forgotten something and whether he had put everything in order. He couldn't forget his son's look of disgust and indignation when he had pulled out his father's sock from under the couch. He didn't take a full breath until he rounded the corner. Proportional to how long it needed to last, today it was from head to toe. Today it was for a week. He had a whole week, he had a conference . . . They used to say that as boys. What did you do yesterday? Yesterday? Yesterday was Saturday. Saturday? I had a conference in Mandalay. He smiled . . . As usual, he had a whiskey at the airport. As usual, it tasted like prom night. Like adulthood. Back then they drank to happiness. Not to contentment, not to health, but to happiness! And then he saw her . . . Actually, movement caught his eye. A plane was taxiing in the distance. And the plane ran over her. She was completely transparent against a huge window. Out of focus between the brightness from outside and the lights from inside. And the plane sent ripples through her. But she was there! Barely perceptible, like an angel . . . He had to get up, he had to go take a look. He shaded his eyes with his hand. And she turned away from the window, from the plane, and got startled. They were standing there, their palms facing . . . And then she smiled . . . maybe . . . and walked away. She left . . . And he didn't turn to look at her. He couldn't move, he was full to the brim. So he just stood there, as if he were made of glass . . . Only when they announced last call . . . he got his things and walked to the boarding area. Carefully, so as not to spill . . . Maybe it's called fate. Or, that's why I'm here. Or, it happened to me, this time it happened to me . . . But he had no idea what she looked like, she must have been beautiful. And then he figured out that he liked her. Because he missed her. Completely inexplicably, he missed her . . . That was how they met. Birds of a feather flock together.

And Pipina and the baby had to go for another vaccination. On the second bus, because who knows why, the first one just flew by . . . zigzagging around dog poo, the occasional spit, through cracks and ditches, underneath frightening, spiky, black graffiti, up crumbling stairs with no other option, but with heaps of cigarette butts . . . Pipina made it to the hospital with the stroller and the baby. But the doctor's office was closed. Out of service, some angry dad hissed under his breath. Everyone was grumbling, but quietly. And they only knocked when there were enough of them, so they wouldn't be afraid. The doctor's away, at a conference. The woman who had screwed it up drawled sarcastically. He could have just as easily been reading the newspaper back there, not even a ray of light could have passed by the nurse . . . And somehow Pipina got a cold, a bad one. But the baby didn't, so a week later they had to go back. Up all those crumbling steps with no other option, but with heaps of cigarette butts . . . And they forgot a handkerchief. It would have been better had they forgotten their heads! Understandably, Pipina didn't want to blow her nose on the two spare diapers, so she looked for leaves. But there was only one tree in front of the hospital entrance. All alone. And that was a giant mistake. But Pipina didn't realize it until it was too late. Until after she had already blown her nose and wiped her face as much as she could and then some, on a couple of the biggest leaves. She even wondered why the tree was losing its leaves, it must be sick, good thing it's right by a hospital . . . It took her a minute before she started to look around nervously, and a moment later she realized she was the one who stank. As usual. And another dog was lifting its hind leg. It was the only tree far and wide . . . And then she heard the bass right behind her, may I help you with the stroller?? Pipina didn't have good luck in life . . . And all three of them were riding the elevator, it was working again. Pipina didn't have a lick of luck in her life. A moment later the doctor shifted his weight from one foot to the other, something stinks in here . . . And upstairs, they clumsily wrestled the stroller off the elevator, one from one end, the other from the other. Thank you. You're welcome. I just need to put on my lab coat and wash my hands. And the bass backed up, you're my first patient today, and he closed the door behind himself . . . The whole time Pipina had only seen him from the waist down. She didn't have the strength to look up. And the baby started to cry, and she started to look for something to wipe her nose, maybe a piece of paper under the benches. Come in, the bass said to a large, protruding posterior. Pipina had awful luck in life . . . And then they had to go in, and out of her tight throat Pipina mustered, may I also . . . Pardon me?? Came a cautious response. May I also wash?? The doctor understood, but didn't put two and two together. Go ahead, he said tentatively. And the baby screamed bloody murder like the first, but as it turned out, not the last time, and Pipina headed for the sink. She was scrubbing her hands, washing her face, and a ray

123

of sunlight caught her leg . . . And Pipina peeked through the gap between the sink and her breasts, more precisely, her chest, small breasts, but a huge butt, everything's connected, and she froze. Toes with painted toenails were sticking out of a sandal. Pipina tried to catch her breath as well as a towel. The last time she had painted her nails was for the wedding . . . She turned around, and the doctor with the baby were looking right into her face. They weren't saying anything, nor were they crying. It was Pipina who was teary eyed from the soap . . . The doctor and the baby looked at one another and then back at her, and little lights went off in their eyes. They were looking at her up close and both exactly the same way! But Pipina didn't see it, her eyes were full of soap . . . The doctor lifted his hand, perhaps he wanted to remind Pipina of the towel. Pipina's hand flew up too, she must have been startled. They stood there with their palms facing. And then the bass said, we know each other, we met at the airport . . . Pipina used to go there because it had direct bus service. While the baby was sleeping, she watched aeroplanes, she watched self-confident, clean people, and what was in fashion . . . They stood there with their palms facing, and she remembered. The man who had smelled so good that nothing even crossed her mind, even though a pig only dreams about corn. And ever since then I've missed you inexplicably, the bass added . . . And Pipina lifted her stinging eyelids until she saw a mouth. He's the one who can fly . . . And he, he wanted to touch her shaking hand, but it hid behind her back. But the baby couldn't take it any more and said brrrr . . . And a little laugh splashed out of each of them, and Pipina's other hand, her right, peeked out from behind her back. And he moved the baby to his left arm, and they touched . . . And he held her until she remembered and said her name. The exact same name her awful mother had had . . . And doctor Norbert Fuxberger said,

Doctor Norbert Fuxberger. And Pipina's achy eyes climbed up to his, I know . . . And they let go, and Pipina closed her hand to hold on to that touch and wrapped her other hand around it . . . And then the doctor vaccinated and put the baby into the stroller. And no one so much as peeped. Not a peep. It was one, long, solemn, quiet moment. Forever . . .

And they lived happily every after. The first time under a roof window. Rain was tapping on it. Some of the droplets managed to slip by, they hadn't had time to close it. Her whole face was salty. Her head hanging off the bed, touching the ground. I'll never forget or regret this . . . A long time ago she had been horrified to hear somewhere . . . an old git had said, a nice pussy often goes unused because of an ugly mug, so she was hoping. She had never looked . . . It's like an orchid, he said. I didn't know you're not supposed to just say it, he said. And now I don't have to envy anyone in this whole lit up housing complex, he said . . . She was happy and she knew it. Finally, at her age, she figured out what an orgasm was . . . And the blinds made stripes on their naked faces, bodies, thighs. How are you? Wonderful . . . Finally I'm in my own skin. Striped! Tiger passion! Don't worry, I won't eat your . . . And then with the last of her strength she whispered, we're neither black nor white, we're striped citizens of our Homeland, and she fell asleep . . .

And he also dreamed. He couldn't remember the last time that happened to him, but it was quite a realistic dream. He dreamed that he knew what would happen in ten years. And he could choose from three options. And all of them were great . . . The baby liked options one and three best . . .

125

TRANSLATOR'S NOTES

PAGE 54 | *luft*: air. From the German *Luft* meaning the same.

PAGE 97 | *Nekem monďa peštinek*: From the Hungarian phrase 'Nekem mondod, pestinek, hogy csíp a poloska?' meaning 'Are you telling me, a person from Budapest, how a bed bug bites?' Figuratively, it means that there is no need to explain the obvious. However, a typical Slovak speaker, like Pipina, would not understand this sentence.

PAGE 102 | *fírhang*: curtains. Dialectal Slovak word.

PAGE 102 | *francle*: decorative tassels. Dialectal Slovak word.

PAGE 102 | *štokerlík*: low stool. Dialectal Slovak word.

PAGE 102 | *hokerlík*: Another dialectal Slovak word for low stool.

PAGE 102 | *fijók*: drawer. From the Hungarian *fiók* meaning the same.

PAGE 102 | *šuflík*: drawer. Dialectal Slovak word.

PAGE 102 | *pakšaméty*: things/stuff. Dialectal Slovak word.

PAGE 102 | *zicherajsky*: safety pins. Dialectal Slovak word.

PAGE 102 | *karperecka*: bracelet. Dialectal Slovak word.

PAGE 102 | *fertig*: done. From German *fertig* meaning the same.

PAGE 102 | *lapítka*: thin article of clothing. Dialectal Slovak word.

PAGE 112 | Loprais wins the Dakar Rally: The Dakar Rally is a rally raid, also known as a cross-country rally, an off-road endurance event that has been organized annually since 1979. Karel Loprais was a Czech rally-raid driver and a six-time winner of the Dakar Rally in the truck category.